Wakefield Libraries
& Information Services

This book should be returned by the last date stamped above. You may renew the loan personally, by post or telephone for a further period if the book is not required by another reader.

7 0 0 0 0 0 0 0 2 5 6 9 7 2

BADLANDS BUCCANEER

To an outlaw like Joel Kelly, a fat payroll would be irresistible. So the railroad detectives baited their ambush carefully. Sacks bulging with gold were loaded on the train. Then the news was 'leaked' so Kelly would hear it.

But in addition to the bullion, armed agents disguised as passengers were planted in the cars. This time, Joel Kelly—the West's most notorious buccaneer—would be cut down in a murderous crossfire of singing bullets.

But Joel Kelly knew exactly what the detectives had planned . . .

BADLANDS BUCCANEER

John Hunter

GUNSMOKE

First published by Ward, Lock

This hardback edition 2001
by Chivers Press
by arrangement with
Golden West Literary Agency

ISBN 0 7540 8154 0

British Library Cataloguing in Publication Data available.

Printed and bound in Great Britain by
BOOKCRAFT, Midsomer Norton, Somerset

Badlands Buccaneer

Chapter One

ON APRIL 3, 1889, Marcomb Sawyer registered at the Antler Hotel in Whitewater, Wyoming. This is a matter of record. The dog-eared ledger with his bold signature still exists. It is not an elaborate register, but then it wasn't an elaborate hotel. Nor for that matter was it in much of a town.

Sawyer was a tall man, and the ceiling of the Antler's lobby was scarcely eight feet above the floor. Milled lumber was hard to come by in that country, and the builders wasted as few feet as need be when they erected the two-story hotel.

Sawyer was tired. He had ridden one hundred and eight miles by stagecoach, and he now looked forward with relief to even the doubtful comfort of the lumpy hotel bed.

As it happened, he was fated not to go to bed at all that night, but he was not yet aware of this. Marc Sawyer, which was not his real name but one he happened to be using at the time, was among the most skillful railroad detectives the United States had ever produced.

In a period when our better trains ran so slowly that a determined horseman could catch up with the average mail car, the number of train robberies was of serious magnitude.

This was a natural enough development. Highwaymen had held up stagecoaches all over the early West, and the mere fact that mail and express were now transported by train did not alter the ambitions of the bandits. Had it not been for Marc Sawyer and men like him, who spent their lives run-

1

ning down the thieves, the losses would have been much greater than they were.

In all his years of service Sawyer had never been pitted against as shrewd, as ruthless, and yet as sporting a character as Joel Kelly.

Kelly was not this road artist's real name. The stories about the gang leader's origin are numerous. It has been told that he was the son of a Mormon bishop and was driven to crime by the persecution of an unsympathetic Federal government. Another story claims that he was the Harvard-educated illegitimate son of a United States Senator and turned to crime through bitterness when his father refused to recognize him publicly.

Marc Sawyer had heard all the stories. He did not know if any were true, and he did not care. Two things he did know. Kelly was educated, and he did have Boston connections, which might well mean that he was a former Harvard student. One of these connections had enabled him to sell three hundred horses to the Boston Horse Car Company, and all of these horses had been found to be stolen.

Kelly was a man of many parts. Unlike the average bandit plying his trade in the badlands of the West, Kelly was a shrewd operator and businessman who spent more time in establishing markets for his stolen goods than he did in robbery itself.

Sawyer's immediate interest in Kelly was concerned with the series of holdups at the time disrupting traffic on the Pacific Northern Railroad.

Like Butch Cassidy and others of the Wild Bunch, who made the Hole-in-the-Wall country their headquarters and used the Outlaw Trail to travel freely between Canada and the Mexican border, Kelly considered the railroads his natural prey. He held up trains at will, and he seemed to have an uncanny ability to guess which trains carried money shipments and which were not worth the trouble of stopping.

Sawyer was not the first operative assigned to the task of corralling Kelly. Many others had tried without success to bring the bandit to heel. And Marc did not have any false notion that the job would be easy.

The country in which Joel Kelly operated was in a state of near anarchy. What law it had known had been largely destroyed by the infamous Johnson County war, which saw the large ranchers and absentee cattle owners pitted against the smaller homesteaders. It had been a period of high-handedness and senseless bloodshed, during which imported gun crews stalked the land.

Some of these men had been rounded up and hanged, but a larger number had taken to the rocky hills and merged into a dozen bands, ranging through a wide territory, sometimes combining for a daring raid, at other times quarreling violently among themselves.

They appeared in town openly, flaunting their contempt for the helpless law officers, daring the sheriff to raise a hand against them, immune to arrest because the people of the country and the local businessmen refused any assistance in their prosecution.

Marc Sawyer knew all this, and he did not make the mistake of revealing either his identity or his reason for being in Whitewater by asking questions he knew would not be answered. In his bold hand, beside his name, he wrote *Whiskey Salesman*. In his two heavy grips he carried bottles, samples of the line he was supposed to represent.

It was a good cover. The bars and saloons were the clubhouses, the meeting places, for two thirds of the nearly womanless population. It was common practice for drummers who handled spirits to treat their prospective customers, and it was natural enough for them to linger and trade gossip with the men they were trying to sell.

Bart Gore was taking care of the hotel desk that night while his brother Frank handled the bar, off the lobby to the right. He reversed the worn ledger and read Sawyer's name slowly, spelling out each letter with his moving lips. Then he looked up.

"New to the business, ain't you? Don't recall seeing you through here before."

"New to this territory," Sawyer said easily. "We never tried to push our line this far west before. I've been working eastern Pennsylvania."

Gore's sullen face lighted. He was a man in his early forties, soured by a life that had not brought him the comforts he wanted.

He ran an unclean hand over the stubble on his square chin. "Come from Philadelphia myself. Ain't been back in ten years." He began to question Sawyer eagerly about the city and about a number of bar owners he had known.

Sawyer answered readily. Before starting on the assignment he had carefully covered the territory with one of the distillery's regular salesmen. An experienced agent made his cover occupation as authentic as possible. Sawyer had not expected to run into an ex-Philadelphian in Whitewater, but he breathed more freely because he had taken the possibility into consideration and primed himself accordingly.

If he had fumbled, if he had failed to answer Gore's questions, the man's suspicions would have been aroused, and that was the last thing Sawyer wanted. He answered everything the man asked and glibly rattled off the first names of several men Gore had forgotten. Tired as he was, he spent a good ten minutes relating the gossip from the Quaker City before he turned toward where he had left his grips, at the foot of the open stairs, his room key in his hand. He had almost reached them when the lobby door opened and a girl came in from the windy street.

Sawyer stopped. The sharp mountain air had put vivid color into her cheeks, but it was not her beauty that captured his attention so much as her clothes. They would have been very much in place in Boston or New York but looked foreign in this raw, undeveloped land.

The same was true of her carriage. She walked with a steady self-confidence yet with no trace of arrogance. She had not been born in the cattle country, that he knew, and the question of what such a woman was doing in Whitewater at once pricked his curiosity.

She glanced at him, then away, as if he were only another piece of the scarred lobby furniture. But there was no offense in this. It was as if she had not seen him at all, as if she was so preoccupied with her own affairs that she was not conscious of his existence.

In the moment when he caught a full view of her, before she turned her head and moved on to the desk, he saw a finely chiseled face that could have been a sculptor's masterpiece, hair that was dark yet soft, its strands curling beneath the edge of the scarf she wore bound around her head against the buffeting wind, and eyes that were blue yet seemed purple at the same time.

Sawyer caught his breath. He had known many women. He was a man, with a sharp lust for life and living, and had taken what pleasures he could where he found them. But here, in this moment, this girl had captured his imagination and desire. There was a haunting quality about her, as if life had already laid a heavy hand across her slender shoulder.

He knew a sudden, intense urge to hear her speak and lingered purposely, bending over his grips and pretending to adjust one of the straps.

"Any word?" There was a husky urgency in the deep-throated tone, yet her voice was musical.

"No word, Miss Kelly."

The name almost jerked Sawyer upright. He managed to master his surprise and slowly undid the strap of his grip. He would not have left now for worlds. His back was toward the desk, and he was nearly a dozen feet away. If they had lowered their voices, he would have been unable to hear, but they either were unconscious that he was still in the room or didn't care if they were overheard.

"But he'll come?" Again the note of desperate urgency. "You said that he would come."

"He'll come." Gore's voice was confident. "He probably hasn't had my message yet. He might be away from camp. He might be anywhere." The hotel man laughed. "It's hard to know where he is. He travels around, you know."

She murmured "Thank you" and headed for the stairs, and

it was no accident that Sawyer, hefting both his heavy bags, straightened just as she came abreast of him and turned so that his broad shoulder nearly knocked her off her feet.

He dropped both bags, twisted to grab her before she fell, then held her gently but firmly.

"I'm terribly sorry." He knew Bart Gore was watching in open-mouthed surprise. "I didn't see you coming."

She recovered her balance. "It's perfectly all right." Her voice still had its husky quality, but now her tone was one of clipped dismissal.

Sawyer released her. He took off his hat. "Believe me, I have never felt quite so stupid in my life." He gave her a small boy's grin. "Honest, I don't usually go around bumping into ladies."

Her face relaxed a little. "I said it was all right. I am not hurt." She took a tentative step away from him.

"I'm Marc Sawyer," he told her, "representing the Old Reliable Distillery of York, Pennsylvania. If I can help you in any way . . ."

"Nothing," she said. "I need no help." She moved quickly to mount the stairs.

Sawyer watched until she reached the upper floor, then turned to find Bart Gore looking at him with thinly veiled dislike. He used his grin again, but it had no noticeable effect on the man.

"I feel like a fool, bumping into a lady like that."

He hoped that Gore would loosen up, perhaps tell him who she was. The hope was vain.

"I wouldn't know," the hotel man said. "I never bumped one."

All the friendliness he had shown during their gossip about Philadelphia was gone from his face, and he watched Sawyer with an intentness that made the agent nervous.

He turned and climbed the stairs. The hotel room was like a hundred others he had occupied, narrow, cell-like, with a frayed carpet, a battered dresser and washstand, a single straight chair, and a swayback bed.

The paper on the walls had been a rose print, but age and

dirt and careless men had marred it until it was hard to tell the original color.

The room had not been used recently, Sawyer judged from the stale air. He raised the single window. Outside, the evening was filled with fine swirling dust kicked up by the restless wind, which flapped the name board of the barber shop next door and made the building around him creak.

But even the dust was preferable to the lack of oxygen that had nearly smothered him when he had opened the door, and for several minutes he stood at the window filling his lungs before he turned back and began to remove his coat and shirt.

Standing naked, he sponged his body with the help of a towel dipped in the tepid water he had poured from the pitcher. When this was done he found his razor, stropped it carefully, and shaved. He had not intended shaving this night, but the meeting with the girl and the possibility that he might be lucky enough to see her again had made him change his mind.

Still naked, he stood before the mirror, blurred in many places where the mercury coating had come free of the back, and studied himself. He was thirty years old, but neither the body nor the face betrayed the age.

The body was powerful, a massive chest tapering to a slim flatness at the hips, a suggestion of bulge about the waistline, but only a suggestion.

His hair was dark and held a curl that comb and water failed to straighten entirely, and his mustache, heavy after the fashion of the time, curled a little at the ends of its own volition.

Without vanity, he knew that he was good-looking and that he had an animal magnetism that women found attractive. He had used this to his advantage more than once for both his own pleasure and the company's business, for above all, Marc Sawyer was a realist.

Had someone questioned his honesty, he would have been surprised. He had never cheated at cards or put his hand in another man's pocket, yet as an undercover agent he had joined a dozen gangs and in the majority of cases brought them to justice. That he had employed trickery in doing so he would not dispute, but to him the end justified the means. He was dedicated to his profession and to the men for whom he worked, and he knew that he would not hesitate to employ the same tactics again no matter what it involved or whom it hurt.

He whistled softly as he dressed. The bath had revived him, and the nagging weariness that had enveloped him when he entered the hotel was gone.

He dressed carefully. There was within him a fancy for fine clothes, and he indulged it whenever it did not interfere with his business activities.

His gun, small by frontier standards, lay on the bed where he had tossed it when he removed it from his grip. He hesitated, then picked it up and returned it to the case. He seldom carried a gun unless the part he was playing made the omission noticeable.

Although proficient in its use, having spent long hours in diligent practice, he much preferred to entrust his safety to his quickness of wit than to his quickness of hand.

Still whistling, he picked up his hat, blew out the single lamp, and stepped almost silently into the hall.

He stopped a moment, listening. The building was constructed in the form of a rectangle just wide enough to accommodate the two rows of rooms opening on the central corridor. Halfway toward the front, the stairway made a railed well, narrowing the hall at that point so it was not wide enough for two people to move abreast.

He passed the well, paused again to listen to the faint sounds that rose from the dining room across the lobby from the bar, and then continued to the door letting onto the upper gallery.

The door stuck a little, and he pulled it inward, assisted by the force of the wind, and stepped out into the darkness, closing the door behind him.

Enough light came from the distant moon to assure him that the gallery was deserted, and he walked forward to rest his powerful hands on the high rail and gaze up and down the street.

Everything below him seemed to be in motion, pushed by the constant impulse of the hoydenish wind. That wind, he well knew, was a permanent part of the country; it blew oftener than it was still.

Dust and scraps of paper and dancing weeds added a thickness to the air. The horses along the rail paid no attention, too used to the agitation to even lift their patient heads.

The town made a checkerboard pattern before him. It was far from large, but for that section of the country it boasted an unusual number of substantial buildings; a cow town, nothing more, drawing its substance from the surrounding ranches and from the many outlaws who used it as their supply point.

There were only a handful of people on the street, and aside from the twenty bars, the business houses were already closed. Sawyer was about to turn back into the hotel and seek his supper when new sound rolled in from the north, a whisper at first, which grew until he could distinguish the drum of half a dozen horses coming down the street.

There were, in fact, seven riders, and they pulled into the rail directly below him, swung down to snub their ponies, and mounted the hotel steps.

In the wide band of light thrown from the lobby's front windows, he studied them, nondescript men, mostly bearded, wearing sheep-lined or blanket coats against the wind's raw edge. They might have been riders from one of the ranches or members of any of the outlaw gangs, but he knew suddenly with a quickening pulse that they were Kelly's men, for Joel Kelly was the first man to dismount, the first man to reach the porch steps.

There were in existence nineteen known pictures of Joel Kelly. If the bandit had a major weakness, it was his fondness for having his picture taken, and he seldom visited a town large enough to boast a photographer without having a likeness made.

Sawyer had studied them all with care, engraving on his

memory every characteristic of the man, and he was certain of his identification now.

Kelly was a little under average height, small-boned, and graceful. But there was nothing feminine about him, and it was rumored that he had abnormal strength in his slender hands. His hair was black, his eyes dark, his nose a little aquiline, and in a period when most men considered it effete to go without hair on their face, he was clean-shaven.

He had another characteristic. In a land that tended to large hats with wide, curling brims, he wore an "iron hat," or derby. He was wearing one now as he stepped up to the level of the lower porch. He passed from Sawyer's view, his men trailing after him.

Sawyer drew a cigar from his pocket, bit off the end, and put it into his mouth, but he did not light it. He stood in the darkness thanking his luck. He believed in luck as fervently as any gambler, and in a sense he was one of the greatest gamblers of them all, for he sat constantly in a game in which his life was the stake, in which one slip, one error, would almost certainly bring death.

It gave him a warm feeling to know that his luck was working for him now. He had expected to have to wait a week, perhaps a month, before he managed to make contact with Kelly, and he had considered this seriously, wondering how to account for a whiskey salesman's lingering so long in one small town.

He could have pretended illness and gone to bed, apparently too sick to move on. But the idea, especially after he saw the hotel room, had little promise of comfort. Now, if his luck held, the case might take only a few days.

He turned, the unlighted cigar still between his pressed lips, walked back through the door and into the empty upper hall, and paused.

The noise from below stairs had increased, and he judged that Kelly and his men had already gone in to supper. In one small detail he was wrong. He descended to find Kelly still in the lobby, seated in a far corner, the girl Sawyer had seen earlier beside him.

Her back was toward Sawyer as he came down the stairs, and she was talking earnestly, almost angrily. Sawyer would have liked to overhear what she was saying, but as he reached the floor level Kelly's eyes came up to meet his.

He looked away, not too hastily, walked over and dropped his cigar into one of the battered brass cuspidors beside the desk, and then moved on into the dining room.

Bart Gore was still behind the desk. He watched Sawyer until he passed from sight and then glanced at Kelly, trying to catch his eye, but the bandit was listening intently to what the girl beside him was saying.

In the dining room a huge table stretched the full length of the narrow, hall-like space. The table could seat a good thirty, and it was already two-thirds full. If the townsmen and drummers resented sharing the table with Kelly's men, they gave no sign, and the outlaws were scattered along both sides of the board, joking with the storekeepers, very much at ease. Only their clothes and the fact that each wore at least one gun set them apart.

Sawyer found a seat near the end of the table beside a big black-haired giant who stood six feet six inches tall and weighed at least two hundred and fifty pounds.

The man ate busily with both hands, as if he feared that one could not convey enough food to his mouth. He glanced at Sawyer and said with his mouth well-filled, "Stranger, huh?"

Sawyer gave him his small, friendly grin. "That's right."

"Drummer?"

"Whiskey salesman."

"Well, by God!" The big man had a bone clenched in his right hand, from which he had been busily gnawing the meat. Now he laid it on the oilcloth table cover and extended greasy fingers.

"Whiskey salesman, huh? Always wanted to meet up with one of you fellows. Got any samples with you?"

"In my room, upstairs."

"You hear that, Fred?" the big man appealed to one of his

companions directly across the table. "Gent's a whiskey drummer, and he's got samples."

Fred had red hair and a narrow, ferretlike face. His squinted eyes were blue-green, and when he smiled his teeth showed, broken and stained.

"Always said a dude was good for something."

The big man turned as the waitress, a heavy woman of middle age, appeared with a fresh dish of potatoes and a platter of meat.

He slapped her affectionately on the behind, so hard that she nearly dropped the food.

"Damn you, Jumbo. You do that again and I'll comb your hair with a dish."

Laughter welled up out of the depths of his big stomach, and his elbows, on the table, shook it so that it threatened to come apart.

"Honest, Florie, you're a card. I swear to God I'd ride a hundred miles through snow just to hear you talk. Come on, give us a kiss."

Across her arm hung the wet towel she had been using to clean the oilcloth at the places of the diners who had finished and gone. She brought it around in a full swing, catching him squarely across the mouth.

A howl of mirth rose up through the room, and she turned and disappeared through the kitchen door, her back rigid with anger.

Sawyer noticed that no one laughed harder than the big man. He nearly rolled from his chair, and his eyes filled with tears of pleasure as he threw one great arm around Sawyer's shoulders, perhaps in a comradely gesture, perhaps merely to steady himself.

"Did you see it?" he gasped when he could manage to speak. "That Florie. There ain't one like her anywhere. I swear to Jesus there ain't. Wouldn't guess she was my girl, now would you?"

Sawyer shook his head.

"Fact." The eyes, which seemed too small in the red

windburn of his face, were suddenly solemn and unsmiling. "Feels real good on a cold night. Might even marry her sometime."

He returned to his eating abruptly, as if fearful he would not get his full share, and in the ensuing pause Joel Kelly came into the room, the girl at his side.

Kelly glanced around and then moved to the head of the table, the girl taking a chair on his right. As if by signal, all conversation ceased.

Florie came back from the kitchen with hot dishes, which she placed at Kelly's elbow. He served the girl, then himself. Sawyer watched him without appearing to. Kelly ate silently, rapidly, as though eating was a chore that failed to interest him but must be accomplished.

There was almost a daintiness in the way he ate, and certainly in contrast to the others at the table his manners were excellent.

The girl barely touched her food, playing with it, eating hardly at all. She did not look up, and the only sign she gave of being aware of her surroundings was to bend her head a little toward Kelly when he spoke to her, in a voice too low to reach Sawyer's ears.

Several of the men had finished eating, but no one stirred from his place until Kelly rose and helped the girl from her seat. They returned to the lobby, and there was a general shifting of chairs as the other diners rose.

Under cover of the confusion Sawyer said, "Pretty, very pretty."

The big man looked at him.

"Who is she?"

All the good humor at once was gone from the heavy face, and the eyes glinted. "Stranger, you don't ask questions about her, and I don't ask questions."

Sawyer pretended deep surprise. "Did I say something wrong?"

The big man studied him for a long minute. Then he relaxed, and a smile again twisted the bloated lips.

"That's all right. You didn't know no better. Let's you and me and Fred go up to your room and have a look at those samples." He licked his mouth. "Course I'm not a drinking man, but I do take a small nip now and then."

Chapter Two

AFTER half an hour Sawyer wondered if he would have any samples left to show the bartenders of the town. No mean drinker himself when the occasion was right, he had never seen anyone drink liquor as rapidly and with as little apparent effort as this Jumbo Wilson.

Still, he did not begrudge the man the two bottles he had already emptied. This was a far better break than he had expected. Where it would lead him he did not know, but already he was on speaking terms with two members of the gang.

It was Fred Kirk who saved his samples. Kirk had confined himself to two drinks, and as Jumbo emptied the second bottle and tossed it noisily into the corner, he said in a warning voice, "Remember what Joel told you. No one gets drunk tonight."

The big man stared at him. His eyes were a little bloodshot, but it was the only sign that he had already consumed enough alcohol to floor two ordinary men.

"Who's getting drunk?"

"You aren't, yet, but we've got a whole evening to kill. Come on, let's go downstairs."

They went downstairs, into the Antler bar. The place was

full, and a curtain of blue smoke hung like a shroud over the gathering.

At the bar Sawyer reached for his pocket, but Jumbo stopped him. "My treat. I been drinking your samples." He pulled out a roll of bills nearly as big as his fist. He saw Sawyer's eyes widen, and chuckled.

"There's easier ways of making money than peddling whiskey."

"Seems so." Sawyer accepted his drink and downed it, noting that the product was not so good as the bottles he carried. "Well, I never had that kind of luck. Always had to work for my money."

"Meaning I don't?" Jumbo's big face clouded.

Sawyer shrugged. "Look, friend, I wasn't trying to offend you, but I'm not exactly dumb, either. I may never have been in this part of the country before, but I do have some general idea of what a cowboy is paid."

Jumbo relaxed. "Say, you're not bad." There was an admiring note in his voice. "I like you. I like you plenty." He raised his enormous hand to slap Sawyer's shoulder. The blow was supposed to be playful. It nearly knocked Sawyer down.

A man came up behind Jumbo. "Kelly wants you."

Without a word the big man swung around and walked out of the barroom. Sawyer watched him go with mixed feelings. He found Jumbo's company a little wearing, but he felt that he had established some contact with Kelly's outfit and he was afraid that whatever he had gained would slip away.

His impulse was to go upstairs to bed. Suddenly all the weariness of the early evening was upon him again. But he resisted the impulse and decided to wait in the bar for an hour on the off chance that Jumbo Wilson would return.

At least he could get off his feet. With this in mind he turned toward the rear of the room, where six poker tables made an irregular pattern.

There were games at four of the tables, and he found a seat at the one in the corner.

The game was not large, and he handed the dealer a twenty-dollar goldpiece, and received change. Cards were not one of his stronger loves, but years of experience had turned him into a better-than-average, if cautious, player.

He had been in the game an hour and had won nearly fifty dollars when something made him look up. It was the feeling of being watched. Most animals have, to an acute degree, a kind of sixth sense that warns when alien eyes are upon them.

Sawyer had the same sense and he looked around quickly, and his eyes met those of Joel Kelly, who was standing at the upper end of the bar beside Jumbo Wilson.

Sawyer did not make the mistake of looking away too quickly, of showing nervousness or fright. He met Kelly's stare levelly, and it was the bandit leader who first looked away. Not until then did Sawyer turn his attention back to the cards.

He played four more hands before shoving back his chair. There were protests from around the table since he was the only winner, but he ignored them, gathering up the money he had won, stuffing it into his pocket, and then turning toward the bar.

Only after he made this turn was he certain that Kelly was still there, still watching him. The knowledge sent a little shiver of apprehension along his spine. He shoved it away consciously. This was exactly what he wanted, that Kelly should notice him, that the man should be interested in him. But he did not want that interest to develop into suspicion, for Kelly could be as dangerous as a cornered wolf.

There was no record that Kelly himself had ever killed anyone, although there were rumors. But it was an established fact that he had ordered the execution of several of his men who had attempted to double-cross him and that two of the agents sent out to trap him had vanished into the badlands.

Sawyer reached the bar half a dozen feet from where Kelly and Wilson stood, turned and nodded in recognition to the big man, and ordered his drink. Wilson did not return the nod. Instead he bowed his head slightly, as if listening to something Kelly was saying. Then he moved down the counter to plant himself directly before Sawyer.

He stood silent, a scowl on his heavy face, his eyes agate-hard as they stared into Sawyer's.

The small hairs at the back of Marc Sawyer's neck rose, and he steeled himself for the blow he thought was coming. Not that he stood any chance in a fight with Wilson. The man could break him easily with his bare hands. Sawyer had no gun, but even a gun would have been useless. Kelly's men were scattered throughout the crowded room.

He made his voice steady by sheer will power, wondering as he spoke what had gone wrong, how he had betrayed himself.

"Drink?"

For a long moment Wilson's expression did not change. Then he said, "Boss wants to see you. Come on." He did not wait for Sawyer's answer. He turned on his heel and marched back to Kelly.

Sawyer took his time finishing his drink. He was shaking inside. Then he paid the bartender and followed Wilson. In that moment he realized that the whole thing had been staged, that Kelly for some reason had wanted to see how he would react under pressure. His opinion of the bandit, already high, rose a notch.

When he reached the two men he paused, looking first at Wilson as if for instructions, then at Kelly, his expression a little puzzled, a little questioning, as if he did not know what this was all about.

Wilson was smiling now, and he sounded friendly. "I was telling the boss about your samples. He hasn't had a taste of good liquor in a long time."

Sawyer watched the bandit leader. Now that he was close he saw that Kelly's eyes were larger than he had realized, soft and candid as a child's.

"I'll be glad to bring some down."

Kelly said, "Don't bother." His voice was as soft as his eyes, and it had a musical quality. There was something about the man that Sawyer liked at once. It was hard to define his charm but it was real, and had he met the man without knowing his history he would have been drawn to him.

"It's no bother."

"I was about to suggest that we go to your room."

"Of course." He grinned in welcome. "That's the ticket. Come on, boys." He nodded and led the way.

Crossing the lobby, he saw from the corner of his eye that from behind the hotel's high desk Bart Gore was watching them with a lively curiosity.

If Kelly and Wilson had noticed this interest, they paid no attention. At the room door he let them pass him, then followed them in, kicking the door shut. Kelly took the single chair as if by right. Jumbo Wilson settled on the bed, which creaked and threatened to give way under his weight.

Sawyer went over and unstrapped one of his bags. He knew as soon as he opened it that it had been searched, for he had carefully placed a hair on top of a white shirt. He stood thinking for an instant, then pulled out a bottle and crossed the room, looking for glasses.

"Best liquor out of Pennsylvania," he told them, "and when you say that you're saying it all. Kentuck never turned out bourbon that can stack up against the whiskey from the Keystone State."

They accepted their glasses, and Sawyer noticed that Kelly sipped his like brandy, while Wilson tossed it down his cavernous throat. He was in the act of pouring a second round when Kelly asked suddenly, "You know who I am?"

Sawyer's head was bent as he poured the drinks, for which he was thankful. He held the bottle steady so that its neck did not clink on the edge of the glass. How should he answer? If he denied knowledge, they would be suspicious; if he showed too much, they would be more so.

"I've got an idea." He finished pouring Kelly's drink and refilled his own.

"Who?"

"Joel Kelly." He raised his glass and drank without looking directly at the bandit.

"What makes you think that?"

Sawyer looked at him and grinned. "Well, I was out on the upper gallery when you boys rode in, and you didn't look exactly like ranchers to me. This afternoon the stage driver was telling one of the other drummers that this is your territory and your town. He told some stories about you. It kind of interested me."

"Why?"

Sawyer's shrug was disparaging. "Shucks, a man like me, traveling around so much, I read a lot. Mostly dime novels. It's kind of different to actually see one of the men they write about." He watched Kelly as he spoke, trying to judge the man, trying to find his weak spot, if he had one. Vanity could well be that spot. The fact that Kelly so enjoyed being photographed was a small indication.

"Then I was sure after I talked to Wilson."

"I didn't say nothing, boss." The big man threw Kelly a worried look.

"Of course you didn't," Sawyer reassured him. "It was the roll of money you were carrying. No cowpoke ever got himself that much money."

"You're pretty smart," Kelly said, cutting him short. "Wilson said you were, and he doesn't make a mistake very often. Then I watched you playing poker. For a dude you handle yourself well. Where you from?"

Sawyer was on surer ground now. He laughed. "I'm not exactly a dude. I come from Ohio, but I've been West, clear to California."

"Always selling whiskey?"

He shook his head. "Selling, but not always whiskey."

"So the company sent you out here. They going to keep you in this territory?"

Sawyer poured another round of drinks before he answered. "That depends. You see, Old Reliable never pushed their goods west of the Mississippi before. It was kind of my own idea. I figured that just because a man lived in this country and had to buck blizzards and heat and such, there was no reason why he should be forced to drink rotgut for want of something better."

Kelly smiled for the first time. His whole face lighted up. "You're a convincing talker."

Sawyer laughed in return. "That's what a salesman has to be, Mr. Kelly. Way I figured it, I'd make this trip, kind of exploring out possibilities, you might say, and if it paid off, then maybe I'd open an office in Cheyenne or Denver or even Salt Lake and put on salesmen, be a jobber for the whole territory."

Kelly was watching him intently. "Ambitious, aren't you?"

Sawyer swallowed slowly. He did not want to put it on too strong, but he did want to get the point across. "Ten years of working for someone else ain't made me rich and it's not likely to. Most I get out of it is a lot of poor food and having to sleep in beds like that"—he indicated the swaying affair on which Jumbo Wilson still wallowed—"and riding in stagecoaches and mud wagons and getting burnt up in cindery smoking cars. If a man can't do better than that, he's not smart enough to be alive. Me, I aim to get somewhere before I die, if I have to steal it."

Kelly chuckled. "Think you'd like riding with us?"

"No sir."

The bandit had not expected such a prompt rejection, and his mouth tightened. "What's the matter, got religion? Figure you're too good to associate with thieves?"

"It's not that," Sawyer said, and looked at him squarely to show that he was not buffaloed. "It's that I don't like riding a horse as well as I like riding a stage. If I've got to be uncomfortable, I prefer to be uncomfortable in a town."

Kelly seemed to lose interest in the conversation. He pulled a cigar from his pocket and inspected the outer wrapping carefully, looking for breaks. Then he bit off the end and lit it, inhaling deeply.

"You interest me. I don't know how much you've heard about me and how we operate."

"Only the stories the stage driver told, and a few things that got in the paper."

"We're different from most of the riders in the brakes. For one thing, they're only stealing to get enough money for grub and whiskey and maybe a woman. Would you believe it if I told you that I've got money in five banks in Europe and South America?"

Sawyer had heard rumors of this, but he shook his head.

"And we're not as cut off from the outside world as you may think. We have agents in Denver and on the coast, in Mexico and even in France and other European countries.

"We need to know what's going on. We need some way of keeping in touch with these people. We need a man who can travel over the country without arousing suspicion. We need a man like a whiskey salesman, say, who can go to any hotel or any city or town and seem to have legitimate business there. How does it strike you?"

Sawyer was staring at Kelly. This suggestion was far beyond his fondest dreams. His chief in the Chicago office had told him, "Go on out to Wyoming. Try to make some contacts. Maybe you can get friendly with some of the lesser members of the gang. Maybe you can even get some of them to talk, so we can find out where Kelly is getting his information about rail shipments."

But this! He had a sudden choking impulse to laugh. He fought it down. This could be a trap, merely an effort to make him betray himself. It did not seem possible that a man as smart as Kelly, a man who had escaped capture for years, would take in an utter stranger on face value and give that stranger the means of collaring him.

The average undercover agent might have snapped at the bait. Sawyer didn't. He took a long time to answer, seeming to study the proposition from every angle. Finally he asked cautiously, "What's in it for me?"

Jumbo Wilson laughed hugely. "Didn't I tell you, boss? Didn't I say he was our boy?"

Apparently Kelly did not hear. He said, "That's pretty much up to you. We'll pay your expenses. Anything you make selling whiskey is of course yours. And you'll get your cut in anything you handle for us."

"Like what?"

"Like telling us when a train is carrying enough boodle to pay us for holding it up."

"And where would I find out a thing like that?"

"You'll learn later, after we've checked on you a little." Kelly stood up. "Ever been in jail?"

Sawyer wished fervently that he had set himself up with a nice criminal record. He hadn't. That had seemed too obvious.

"No, and I don't ever want to be."

Jumbo chuckled. "Boy, I've seen some lulus in my time, bugs that could walk off with the place, bars and all—"

"Shut up," Kelly told him without heat. "We'll check you, Sawyer, and if you're all right, we'll work out a deal you won't regret. But right now I've got a job for you to do whether the rest comes along or not."

Sawyer watched him. "What kind of job?"

"Nothing difficult," Kelly told him. "My sister is here. Maybe you saw her at dinner tonight. She shouldn't have come. She has to go back to Denver, and I don't want her to go alone."

"Why not?"

"Because her husband is waiting for her. I'd go myself, or send Jumbo, but we have business that can't wait."

Sawyer said slowly, "I'd think you'd hesitate, sending her anywhere with a stranger."

There was something wolfish in Kelly's eyes, his smile. "Don't worry. In the first place she's pretty good at taking care of herself. In the second, we know who you are, what you look like, and who you work for. If something I didn't like happened, you couldn't run far enough or hide deep enough to keep from being killed."

He paused, and in spite of himself Sawyer shivered a little. There was a distinct deadliness about Mr. Joel Kelly.

"And third," the man added, "I just offered you something you want, you want very badly. I could tell it by your eyes. All right, do this for me, show me that I can trust you, and the sky will be the limit. Before you're through you can live in Europe like a grand duke."

He nodded, turning toward the door. "Wait here. I'll fetch her."

Chapter Three

MARC SAWYER had never met a woman like Virginia Kelly. All during the long night, as the mud-wagon stage jolted toward Cheyenne, they exchanged hardly a word. It was not until after they changed coaches and were heading down through Colorado that she turned talkative.

They were alone in the body of the coach, dropping off the ridge toward Fort Collins, when she looked at him abruptly.

"You never met my brother before last night, did you?"

Sawyer had been asleep with his eyes open. He came to with a start. "What was that?"

She repeated her question, and he shook his head.

"I never did."

She was studying him frankly now, her black eyes glinting with either amusement or anger. He did not know which, and he was instantly, deeply alert.

"Then, why do you think he sent you south with me?"

Sawyer shrugged. "I got the impression he didn't want you traveling alone."

"You know who he is?"

Sawyer bowed his head.

"And you're working for him?"

"There was some discussion along those lines but no actual agreement."

She leaned forward and tapped his knee with her index finger for emphasis. "You're a fool, Mr. Sawyer. No one ever mixes with Joel Kelly without getting into trouble. And once mixed up with him, you never get free. He sees to that. He absorbs people, eats them, makes them do what he wants done, and then throws them aside."

Sawyer had difficulty in concealing his amazement. "You sound as if you don't like him."

"Like him?" He had never heard such venom in a woman's voice. "I despise him. I loathe the ground he walks on. But we're a curious family, Mr. Sawyer. We've always hated each other. My mother never spoke to my father from the first day I can remember, but they lived together until she died. At least in the same house."

"You were Mormons?"

She glanced sidewise. "You've been hearing some of the stories Joel started. Joel is like an actor. He likes people to talk about him. He also likes to be mysterious. Actually, we were born under Beacon Hill and our name is not Kelly. Never mind what it is."

"I wasn't going to ask."

She considered him again. "You're a strange man. I can't see why you want to get involved with Joel. I can understand someone like Jumbo Wilson. But you're educated. You have culture."

Sawyer was very much on guard now. He knew how dangerous it could be when someone talked without reticence. Maybe this girl hated her brother—or maybe this was merely a way of testing him. It seemed incredible that she could belong to a gang of outlaws, but he had long since learned that women were far more dangerous than men. Women had the ability to seem to be what they were not. Some of the deadliest females in history had a sweet, winsome look that men mistook, much to their sorrow.

He laughed, as if pleased by the flattery. "The reason is short. Money."

She shook her head quickly. "I find that hard to believe."

"Why? Don't you like money?"

"Not enough to want it from certain sources."

"Meaning the way your brother gets his?"

"I didn't say that, but that is exactly what I mean."

He shrugged. "Miss Kelly—"

"I'm Mrs. Floyd Pierson."

"All right, Mrs. Pierson. When you have traveled as many miles as I have, and stayed in a thousand hot, airless hotel rooms, and listened to a thousand customers grouse about the product you are trying to sell, you reach a point at which any chance to acquire enough money to make yourself independent is very attractive."

She said quickly, "That's the point I'm trying to make. Once you throw in with Joel Kelly you will never be independent again. I'm trying to warn you before it's too late."

He stared at her. Certainly she sounded sincere, and she was so attractive. She was the most attractive woman he had ever met. He was tempted to try to kiss her. Alone in the coach, with only the driver on top, there was not too much she could do to repulse his advances. But he checked himself, afraid he would jeopardize what he had already accomplished.

"Why should you bother to warn me? You never saw me before last night."

She was silent for a long moment. Then she bent toward him a little. "Because I have no choice. Because they are going to kill my husband."

This was certainly his day for surprises. "Kill your husband? Why?"

She said, "That isn't the important thing. I came north to see Joel, to try to make him stop, but he paid no attention to anything I said. I even threatened to go to the authorities, and he laughed at me. Who would I go to? The chief of police in Denver? Denver, after New Orleans and San Francisco, is the most corrupt city in the United States."

Sawyer knew this was true. Gamblers, thieves, and confidence men were better protected in Denver than in almost any other city. They ran wide open, not hesitating to show their contempt for those who tried to bring them to justice.

"The United States Marshal? What jurisdiction would he have?"

Sawyer sat back. It was a beautiful trap. All he had to say was "You don't know me, but I'm with the Pacific Northern Railroad. I can reach the men you can't. I can protect your husband."

He did not speak. He had seen many traps like this before, perhaps not as cleverly baited but along the same lines.

"Do you think I have anything to do with this?"

She said slowly, "I don't know. I don't seem to know anything any more." She settled against the seat and closed her eyes as if she were too tired to talk further, leaving Sawyer to nurse his own thoughts, to speculate on what she might try next.

He had not been in Denver in more than four years, and he had little fear that anyone would recognize him. Still, it was the central meeting place for the bad men of the West and it was always possible that someone would spot him.

The Fairview House was only two blocks from the Mint. It was not impressive, despite the red plush furniture with which its lobby was decked. He was not reassured by the clerk who bowed slightly to the girl as they stepped to the desk.

"Welcome home, Mrs. Pierson."

She nodded. "Hello, Gilbert. Is my husband in the hotel?"

"I saw him go into the saloon half an hour ago. I'll have him called."

She nodded again, and a scrubby boy came forward and took her traveling case as she turned to Sawyer.

"Thank you. It was kind of you to help me from the stage."

Sawyer was conscious that the clerk watched him, listening carefully.

"Will I see you again?"

"I think not." She moved away as a slight, brown-haired man hurried from the doorway of the connecting bar.

"Virginia. I didn't expect you until tomorrow."

"I finished sooner than I expected. Shall we go upstairs?"

She made no effort to introduce Sawyer, and this the clerk noted with secret satisfaction.

They stood across the desk from each other as Virginia Kelly and her husband moved to the open stairway and climbed to the second floor.

"Known Mrs. Pierson long?"

"Not long," said Sawyer. "I met her on the stage."

He accepted the pen from the clerk's pale hand and signed his name, but his mind was not on what he was doing. He was fishing back through a carefully ordered memory, trying to recall where he had seen Floyd Pierson before.

"They been here long?"

The clerk had drawn a brass key from a rack on the wall behind him. "Not too long. Six months, maybe."

"Mr. Pierson in business in Denver?"

"He's a gambler." The clerk's tone told that he did not exactly approve of gamblers. "But a square one, so they say. Staying for a while?"

Sawyer's shrug was expressive. He turned and followed the grubby boy up the stairs and along the hall to a room at the back.

When he was alone he sat down on the bed, trying to think. Joel Kelly's instructions had not been very informative. He was to wait in Denver until he heard from the bandit leader. He had no idea how long that would be.

And then, suddenly, he remembered where he had seen Pierson. It had been in Fort Worth, five years before. He could still visualize the hot courtroom, the buzzing flies, the red-faced, shirtsleeved crowd. The Layton boys were being tried for holding up a Texas Pacific train. The witness for the prosecution, the slender, youngish man in the box, had been Floyd Pierson.

His first quick thought was that Pierson would recognize him. Then he dismissed this as improbable. He had been there only as an observer, because the Layton gang had been wanted also for a holdup on the Pacific Northern, and he had not revealed his identity, not even to the local authorities.

No, unless Pierson had seen him on some other occasion the man would not know that he was a railroad detective. But what was Floyd Pierson doing married to Joel Kelly's sister?

He shook his head, having no answer, and stretched out on the swayback bed without undressing. In three minutes he was asleep.

He never knew how long he slept. When he roused, the room was full dark, and he lay for several minutes unstirring. Then he rose, found a match, lit the lamp, and looked at his watch. It was twenty minutes after eleven.

He debated. He was hungry, but he was still tired from his forty-eight-hour stretch without sleep. He had just started to remove his shirt when a knock rattled the door.

He stared at it, still a little groggy. Slowly he rose and reached for his gun. He tucked it into his belt and pulled on his coat.

"Who is it?"

"Me."

He could not identify the voice. He walked to the door and unsnapped the bolt, and pulling it open, saw Jumbo Wilson's broad, reddish face.

"Well, hello."

Wilson came in, swiftly closing the door. "How are you?"

Sawyer watched him without appearing to, his mind busy weighing the man's unexpected appearance. "I thought you had other things to do, that you couldn't come to Denver?"

"Change of plans." The big man's voice was easy. "That's something you'll learn, friend Sawyer. When you work for Joel any plan's likely to be changed at any moment. Come on."

"On where?"

"You ask too many questions." The good humor had disappeared from the big man's voice, the smile from his brown eyes.

Sawyer shrugged. He blew out the lamp as Wilson reopened the door, and followed him into the hall. They moved toward the stairs, and just before they reached them the big man knocked at a door on the right. A man's voice, muffled by the panel, called, "Who is it?"

"Jumbo. Open up."

The bolt was drawn, and Floyd Pierson was in the doorway. He had his boots off, and his shirt, and it was obvious that he had been preparing for bed.

"What do you want?"

"I want you to meet Marc Sawyer. Marc, come here and shake hands with Floyd Pierson. You two will be working together."

Jumbo stood aside, and Sawyer stepped forward, extending his hand. As he did so, a gun exploded behind him. He saw the bullet strike Pierson's bare chest. He saw the man throw up his hands and fall. Instinctively Sawyer caught him, turning his head to say something to Jumbo Wilson in quick anger. But Wilson's gun was in its holster, not, as Sawyer had expected, in his hand. Behind Wilson the door on the other side of the hall was just closing.

"Where'd that shot come from?"

The big man sounded stupefied. "Don't know. Take care of him. I'll get a doctor." He turned and ran down the stairs with a speed surprising for one of his bulk. "I'll get the police."

Sawyer hesitated. The blood from the man's wound was running over him. He got a better hold on Pierson and carried him to the bed.

He heard feet on the stairs, and excited voices. He felt for the man's pulse. Pierson was dead. Sawyer straightened, and behind him heard a cry. Turning, he saw Virginia Kelly in the doorway, saw the desk clerk beyond her, his face white.

The girl gasped, staring past him at her husband's body. Then in a voice as deadly as any he had ever heard, she said, "You killed him. I thought you were different from the rest, but I was wrong. You killed him." She turned blindly and forced her way past the clerk.

He stood frozen, his eyes protruding.

Sawyer started toward him. The man broke and ran after the girl, not heeding Sawyer's command to stop. For an instant Marc Sawyer was immobile; then he crossed the hall with quick strides and tried the opposite door. To his surprise it was unlocked and banged back as he pushed it, hard. The room was unlighted, but the hall bracket lamp above Pierson's door shed some illumination, and as far as he could see the room was empty.

His gun drawn, he moved cautiously into the room. He stooped to peer under the bed, which was the only possible place of concealment. There was no one there.

He hesitated seconds only, then crossed to the window and peered out. As he had expected, there was a fire escape outside it.

He pushed up the window and leaned across the sill to look down at the ill-lighted alley. A shadow moved, and he raised his gun; then the voice of Jumbo Wilson came up to him out of the darkness.

"Sawyer, that you?"

He answered guardedly.

"Come down here quick. I've got him."

Sawyer slid one leg over the sill and stepped out onto the grilled platform, then dropped down the ladder into the blackness at Jumbo Wilson's side.

"Where is he?"

Jumbo Wilson laughed, his chuckle more sinister than any threat. "Friend, he's a mile away by now, and if you're wise you'll be three miles away in like time. I've got horses at the end of the alley, and you'd better be on one of them and traveling fast before that desk clerk gets back with the police."

Sawyer's impulse was to shove his drawn gun against the man's big stomach and pull the trigger. He'd been had. He knew it now. Neatly framed for the murder of Pierson, and he did not need to be told that any story he tried would be laughed out of a Denver court.

"Where's the horses?"

Wilson put out a big hand and squeezed his shoulder almost affectionately. "I told Joel you were smart. Yes sir. You don't have to get hit on the head with an ax to know when you've been taken. Come on, you'll do to ride the river with."

He turned and made his way quickly along the alley, Sawyer at his heels. The horses were good, and fresh. It showed that Jumbo Wilson was not a man who took unnecessary chances. They mounted and headed west, angling northward until they crossed the Platte, then swinging due north.

Sawyer was content to follow. It was obvious that Wilson knew exactly where he was going, that he had ridden there many times before.

They rode in silence until the last scattered buildings of the town had been left behind. Then, after climbing a short grade, Wilson pulled his hard-breathing horse to a halt and eased himself in the saddle as Sawyer drew up beside him.

"Well, friend. You're out and clear, and the chances are you won't have trouble as long as you keep out of Colorado, and as long as you don't ever try to cross Joel and the boys."

Sawyer said shortly, "You went to a lot of trouble to frame me. Was it worth it?"

The fat man's chuckle filled the quiet night. "That's where Joel's different from most of the Wild Bunch. He plans, see. He gets everything set up just the way he wants it before we ever make a move.

"Take tonight, for instance. Three of us rode over three hundred miles just to fix things so you and the law ain't never going to be comfortable again. Joel's a smart man. He doesn't want anyone riding for him who ain't got at least one murder chalked up against him."

Sawyer's shrug was more expressive than words. "So what good am I to him if I've got to hide from the law?"

The big man was surprised. "Who said anything about hiding? Hell, no one's going to go looking for you outside of Colorado unless someone calls attention to you. But we just like to have a handle on a man, something we can hold onto in case he gets cute. That's Joel's idea. Joel's got a lot of ideas. Know what he calls himself? A buccaneer. Know what that is? A pirate, one of those old guys who used to sail around in ships a-murdering and a-robbing."

Still Sawyer did not speak. There seemed to be very little to say.

"So we took care of Pierson and we got you fixed just the way we like, so maybe it was worth riding three hundred miles to do."

"Why Pierson? What did you have against Miss Kelly's husband?"

The big man snorted. "Pierson was asking for it. Know what that skunk was? A railroad detective. Just imagine the gall of the guy, marrying Joel's sister just so he could get his cuffs on Joel. The things those bastards won't try. But it don't do them a bit of good. Joel can smell them out a mile away. That makes six we've taken care of so far, but they never stop trying. I guess they won't until we've killed an even dozen. Come on, let's ride. We've got a long way to go."

Chapter Four

MILTON, Montana, was a boom town. Not because of anything its citizens had accomplished or because the rather barren country around it produced anything of value, but simply because Eastern promoters and moneyed gentlemen in the Puget Sound area had decided to build two railroads and these two lines happened to cross each other at Milton, making it a junction.

Marc Sawyer came into Milton on the first of August. It had been almost four months since he rode out of Denver with Jumbo Wilson. In those four months he had learned as much about Joel Kelly as a man who did not live with the gang leader twenty-four hours a day could know.

He had, during the period, traveled through most of the West, always as a whiskey drummer. He had been careful to detour Colorado, for as far as he knew he was still wanted in Denver for the murder of Floyd Pierson.

The call to Milton had come as a surprise. In the months since he had first met Joel Kelly, he had had no real part in the ring's activities, although on the first of each month he had received two hundred dollars in gold from Kelly, usually delivered to a prearranged spot by Jumbo Wilson.

There had been three train robberies during this time, which he suspected were the work of Kelly's men, but he had no direct knowledge of them and dared not question Wilson. His home office in Seattle was becoming impatient, and he had about concluded that for some reason he had failed to gain Kelly's trust when the summons reached him in Salt Lake. He started for Milton at once.

Sawyer arrived on the late-afternoon stage from the south, then went directly to the Milton hotel, registered, and left most of his luggage in his room. Next, carrying a bag of samples, he went as directed to the Bitterroot Saloon.

It was five o'clock when he got there. A small poker game was being played listlessly at one of the rear tables, but there was no one at the bar except the fat attendant.

Sawyer set the grip on the sawdust-covered floor, then pulled a cigar from his pocket and offered it to the bartender.

"My name's Sawyer, Marc Sawyer. I represent the Old Reliable Distilling Company of York, Pennsylvania, with some of the finest package goods in the trade."

The bartender accepted the cigar, stuck it in his pocket, but his red face did not relax. "Too high-class for us, mister."

"Boss around? Just tell him the man from Pennsylvania is here."

The bartender, who had been turning away, stopped, his manner altering. "Why didn't you say so?" His tone had dropped, and he glanced at the poker players as if he feared they might overhear. "He's in the office now." He jerked his head toward a door in the wall beyond the end of the bar.

Sawyer said, "Thanks," and hefted his grip and moved toward the door. He knocked, and Jumbo's well-remembered voice called, "It ain't locked."

He went in. Joel Kelly sat before the desk, a half pack of cards in his hand, the rest spread out before him. He looked up, nodded, and went on with his solitaire.

Wilson came forward, grinning, to slap Sawyer's shoulder so hard he almost dropped his sample case.

"Hiyah, boy. How's the whiskey business?"

"Fair. My line's a little high-class for this part of the country."

Joel Kelly found the card he wanted in the pack. He played it with an air of triumph, as if the game were the most important thing in the world. Then he tossed the cards onto the desk and looked at Sawyer.

"Ready to go to work?"

Sawyer nodded. At long last he was to get a chance. "I sure am."

"All right." Kelly's voice was crisp. "This should be easy. The Montana Central is building a line south from here. They're about fifteen miles out with their steel, twenty with their grade. They've got two thousand men, and those men haven't been paid in something like thirty days. They make a dollar a day, so that adds up to fifty thousand, in gold." He stopped, watching Sawyer closely.

Sawyer decided to sound impressed. "Fifty thousand!"

"Not a bad day's work." Joel Kelly gave him his quiet, mocking smile. "Now, it's your job to find out when that pay car is coming through from Spokane. The paymaster's name is Croyner, Bob Croyner, and he's a fool. He drinks too much. You find out when the car is due, whether it will be easier to hit it on the Northern, while they're switching here in Milton, or after it's hooked onto the work train for camp."

"How will I decide?"

Kelly reached out, riffled the cards on the desk before him. "Jumbo keeps telling me how smart you are. This is your chance to prove it. If this works, you're on the road."

"And how do I get word to you?"

"Jumbo will be around. You get word to him."

"And where do I find Croyner?"

"He drinks in here every night. Don't talk to Jumbo in public. If you meet him on the street, you don't know him."

"But—"

"That's all." The way Kelly spoke, the slight edge of contempt with which he dismissed Sawyer, stirred Marc's anger.

He stared at the man for a long moment. This little dandy needed someone to take him apart, and it was a job Sawyer would dearly have loved to do. Through the long weeks he had been building up a dislike for the small outlaw that now bordered on hatred. It was rooted in many things—in his contempt for law breakers, in his knowledge that Kelly was waxing rich from his holdups. But more than that it was built on the cold-blooded way Floyd Pierson had been killed, and the careful, relentless planning that had gone into framing him for that murder.

He had to steady himself for a moment, to get the anger out of his voice before he could answer in a normal tone..

"All right. One thing more. What's my cut in this?"

Joel Kelly looked up, and there was a flicker of flame in his dark eyes and the devil carefully screened in his small breast nearly burst into the open. Sawyer would not have been surprised if Kelly had jumped to his feet and struck him. Instead Kelly found a smile somewhere and allowed it to twist his soft, mobile mouth.

"Always looking out for yourself. Pull this off and you get one tenth."

"Five thousand." Sawyer said it aloud, and sounded breathless.

"This is only the start," Kelly assured him. "If you do a good job on this, you'll make five times as much before the year is out. Now find Croyner and start getting acquainted."

Two hours later Bob Croyner walked into the Bitterroot Saloon. The big room had filled up in the interim. Four poker games were going. Men stood three deep at the long counter, and there were three bartenders to serve them.

Croyner was short and heavy-shouldered, his hair just beginning to turn gray. He had been drinking, but as nearly as Sawyer could judge, he was not drunk.

He spoke bluntly to half a dozen men as he came along the bar to find a place at the far end. Sawyer shifted slowly until he managed to ease himself in at Croyner's elbow. He grinned engagingly.

"Some crowd."

Croyner shrugged. "You should see it on Saturday night when the crew comes in from the construction camp. You can't walk along the street."

Sawyer reached down, pulled a bottle from his pocket, and motioned to the nearest bartender. "Set them up for everyone." He turned and raised his voice.

"My name's Sawyer, Marc Sawyer, gentlemen, and I represent the Old Reliable Distillery. We are makers of the finest drinking liquor this country has ever seen. I invite you all to taste our product."

He turned back to find Croyner watching him with slightly bloodshot eyes. "Whiskey salesman, huh?"

"That's right, and my room is full of samples." He winked. "Might be you'd like to accompany me up there after a while? A man must get tired of drinking this swill."

Croyner laughed. "As long as they put it in a bottle I'll drink it."

Suddenly a disturbance rose at the door. Six men had shoved in and now stood there glaring at the crowd. In a loud, high voice the foremost said, "There he is," and the six pushed forward in a wedge.

Croyner came around solidly as the men hauled up behind him and the leader spoke.

"We want to talk to you, Croyner."

Sawyer had turned also. The men were dirt-stained, and he guessed they were workers from the railroad camp.

Croyner said, "Talk, then." He sounded a little contemptuous.

"Outside."

"Here."

They eyed each other for moments in silence. Then the one

who had spoken, who seemed to be the leader, demanded, "When do we get paid?"

Croyner had the small glass of whiskey in his hand. He raised it, drank slowly, and used the back of his hand to wipe his mouth before he said, "I told you. As soon as the car comes."

"That's what you said last week."

"That's what I'll say next week if it isn't here by then."

"Damnit, we want our money. You can stand there and drink, and the men at camp haven't a dime in their pockets."

"It'll be here in a few days."

"That's not good enough. You're going to march over to the station with us. You're going to wire Spokane and tell them that if the car isn't here by tomorrow night the whole crew will walk off the job. And that isn't all. They'll come into this town and wreck all the railroad property in sight."

"Will they?" Deliberately Croyner reached back and set his glass on the bar. Then without warning he hit the taller man squarely on the jaw with a left hook that traveled only half a dozen inches.

The man went down like a shot bird. The action had come so abruptly that it caught the room flat-footed. For an instant the men stood stunned. Then they began shifting quickly out of the way of the coming fight, until Croyner and Sawyer stood alone at their section of the bar, facing the remaining five construction workers across the prostrate body.

For a minute longer the five stood motionless, as if not quite realizing what had happened. Then they charged. Croyner, who appeared to relish the prospect of a fight, plunged forward to meet them.

Sawyer came in at his side, both fists swinging. He took a blow on the head, another to the side, and then someone jumped on his back.

He swung around, loosening the man's hold, and reached behind him to lock his fingers around the man's neck and flip him over his shoulder. The man landed sprawling in the sawdust.

Someone hit Sawyer in the side, nearly flooring him, and

he swung away to face a man charging, head down, to butt him.

He caught the man's hair with both hands, then brought up his knee hard and smashed the man's face down against it.

The man dropped, and Sawyer had a moment to look around. Croyner was down, two men on top of him, one beating at his stomach, the other gouging at his eyes.

Sawyer dragged one off and threw him into the bar. The second tried to roll away, and Sawyer kicked him in the ribs as Croyner came to his feet.

Two of the railroad workers were still upright, but they backed off as Croyner stalked them like a hungry cat, then broke and ran for the door.

Croyner came back. The side of his face was puffed and there was a streak of blood from a cut at the corner of his mouth, but he was grinning happily.

"That'll teach the bums." He did not thank Sawyer for his help. Instead he said, "Come on. I'll buy a drink."

"Why drink this stuff? I've got a lot better in my room."

"What are we waiting for?" Croyner turned toward the door. One of their late assailants was struggling to his knees. Croyner kicked him neatly on the cheekbone, and he fell flat on his face.

In the hotel room Sawyer pulled off his coat, went to the case, and brought out two bottles of whiskey. He uncorked one and handed it to the paymaster, then opened the other for himself and sat down on the edge of the bed.

"Nice quiet town you got here."

Croyner grinned. "That wasn't much of a fight. Boys don't know how to fight nowadays. Should have seen some of the battles we had on the U.P."

"How come they haven't been paid?"

Croyner took a long pull from the neck of the bottle and smacked his lips. "Man, you weren't lying. That's real whiskey, yes sir." He drank again. The bottle was half empty. Sawyer thought the railroader must have a capacity nearly as large as Jumbo Wilson's.

He did not want to repeat his question, and Croyner

seemed to have forgotten it. "You get much business in this
territory?"

"First trip up this way. Figure on staying around a couple
of weeks, maybe. Best way to sell is to get to know all the
saloon owners. Funny thing, man gives his order to someone
he knows quicker than he does simply to get high-class mer-
chandise."

"Wait until after payday." Croyner paused and emptied the
bottle in four swallows. "Saloon men will have gold running
out of their ears. Ain't been much money spent around here
in the last four weeks."

"Why so long?"

Croyner blinked at him, and his speech was a little thicker.
"Company had trouble. They been selling stock and bonds,
and the Seattle banks held up the money some way. Anyhow,
it will be through next week, don't know the day."

"Looks like they'd let you know."

Croyner's shrug was expressive. "Them big boys never tell
us working stiffs nothing. It's me that's got to take the grief."
He was beginning to feel sorry for himself. "You saw what
happened tonight. Third time I've been jumped in ten days.
It's enough to make a man drink." He looked hopefully at
the bottle Sawyer held, which was down only a couple of
inches.

Sawyer extended it. Croyner drank deeply. Finally he set
it aside with regret. "Gotta go. Old lady gives me hell if I
stay out too late." He angled toward the door.

"Night."

"Night." Sawyer sat quietly after the door had closed. He
had made contact with the paymaster. The fight had been a
help. Nothing could bring two men together more quickly
than a shared fight. But what good had it done him? Croyner
had said that the pay car would move sometime next week,
but perhaps Croyner had been saying the same thing for the
last four weeks.

He could telegraph his boss in Seattle, but there was the
danger that Kelly might have one of the telegraph agents in
his pay. No, a better way would be to go to Spokane himself,

set up the whole thing, alert his boss, get enough men on the
train to give Kelly's crew the battle they had coming.

But he dared not leave Milton without first checking with
Jumbo Wilson. He couldn't take a chance on the possibility
of a slip now that they had come so far.

He rose, got his hat, and left the room. He had no idea of
where to find Wilson, no contact other than the fat bartender.

He stepped from the hotel. A train from the East had just
pulled into the depot across the wide street, and he waited
idly, watching the passengers alight.

A girl came down the steps of the third car, carrying a
small bag, hesitated, then moved across the dust ribbon
toward the hotel. He did not recognize her until she entered
the band of light thrown from the lobby windows. He stiffened. It was Virginia Kelly.

His impulse was to duck back into the hotel doorway, but
he was uncertain whether she had recognized him. She came
up on the sidewalk and stopped, staring up at him.

There was no surprise in her face, only a deep loathing in
her voice as she said clearly, "Do you mind getting out of my
way, you murderer?"

Chapter Five

HE stared at her, held by the shock of surprise. The last
person he had expected to meet in Milton was Virginia Kelly.
Sawyer's first impulse was to explain, to try to make her understand that he had been framed, that he had had no more
to do with her husband's death than she had.

Standing there on the dark street of the raw frontier town, he knew suddenly that her opinion of him was the most important thing in the world.

He was analytical enough to realize this was slightly absurd. Actually, he did not know her. Their only real contact had been during the stage trip from Whitewater to Denver.

But something in her personality had struck a spark within him, and he stood wordless before her, still not trusting her, still not free to justify himself.

"I asked you to get out of my way."

Her tone was calm, cool, yet it held a burning undertone of contempt that made him writhe.

He did not move. Long years of playing parts had schooled him in successfully masking his feelings.

"You're the last person in the world I expected to meet here."

"I can guess that much." Her contempt showed more plainly. "And probably the last person you wanted to see. Well, Mr. Sawyer, or whatever you are calling yourself at the moment, you had better be worried about it. I'm going to spend the rest of my life hounding you, no matter where you go."

He didn't answer, but the thought of her chasing him from one end of the country to the other brought a smile to his lips.

She saw the smile and misunderstood its meaning. "Go ahead and laugh. You and my brother think that you are so clever, that you can get away with murder always, that a woman can do nothing to stop you. But you're wrong. In every town you go to, I'll tell the authorities who you are and how you killed my husband. Oh, I know you'll be fairly safe."

Her tone turned more bitter. "No one in Colorado really cares whether you are brought to trial. The whole government there is run by swindlers, by gamblers, by gunmen. But you'll grow tired of having my finger point at you every time you turn around. No matter how bad a man is, he gets tired of running, sooner or later."

He fought down the impulse to reach out, to grasp her

slender shoulders in his big hands, to pull her to him and kiss her thoroughly.

Had someone told him he was in love with her, he would have laughed. He had all the distrust of human relationships that a man playing a lone hand against heavy odds builds up to shelter him from a world he suspects.

But her physical attraction was overwhelming. He wanted her urgently, as he had never believed that he could want any woman.

He said, "How did you find me? Or did you come to see Joel?"

As soon as he had asked the question he could have bitten off his tongue. It was a slip. He realized it as soon as the words had left his lips, even before she said in surprise, "Is Joel here? What devilment are you two up to now?"

He tried to lie convincingly. "He isn't, not that I know of. I only thought that because you showed up he must be in the neighborhood, too."

"That's not very good. Or maybe I know enough now to see through your lies. On that ride to Denver I actually believed that you were a decent person. I really thought that you were a fundamentally honest man who had been trapped by Joel. I was worried for you. I didn't realize that you were merely a killer for hire. What murder are you and Joel planning now?"

He was silent.

"I can guess. In the morning I'm going to warn the sheriff and tell him who you are. I'll go to the railroad officials and tell them that Joel is planning to hold up some train. Good night."

She swept by him, carrying her foldable portmanteau, and disappeared into the hotel.

He stood there. This was a complication none of them had expected. Unless, of course, this was still another of Joel's devious methods of testing him, unless the girl was putting on a stupendous act.

This he refused to believe. He did not think any woman was that good an actress. Yet because he realized he was emotionally drawn to her, he refused to let his mind accept her actions at face value.

But if she were telling the truth, if she had dedicated herself to bringing him and Joel to justice, her presence in Milton could be disastrous to their plans. Let the local railroad officials learn that Joel Kelly and his agents were in the area and they would either delay shipment of the payroll or surround the train with so many guards that Kelly would call off the holdup.

Sawyer swore softly under his breath. Damn women, anyhow, even such attractive ones as Virginia Kelly. They had a genius for complicating things. If this plan failed to come off because of her presence, then he would have wasted the whole four months. And when Kelly learned of his sister's intention of camping on Sawyer's trail, there was a good chance he would not use Marc again.

He pulled a cigar from his coat breast pocket and bit the end off viciously, wondering what he should do. And then it came to him. He could use the girl's presence in town as an excuse not to remain in Milton, as an excuse to go to Spokane.

He grinned. If Kelly was using his sister to check on Sawyer, this would turn the tables on the bandit nicely. If not, no harm would be done. Sawyer had no fear that Kelly would harm the girl. He had watched Joel in the lobby as he had talked with his sister. No matter how they might disagree, it had been obvious that Kelly was both fond and protective of his sister, as long as her activities did not interfere with his. At worst, he would probably get her out of Milton until after the holdup.

Sawyer threw the still unlighted cigar into the gutter, crossed the dusty street, and went into the Bitterroot Saloon.

The room was nearly full and the poker tables were going full blast, although, he noted absently, the play was not very heavy.

Bob Croyner was standing at the bar. As Sawyer came in he twisted his head and motioned him forward. The last person Sawyer wanted to see at this moment was the railroad paymaster, but there was no help for it. He walked over to the counter and allowed Croyner to buy him a drink.

"How's it going? Any more fights with the men?"

Croyner gave him a crooked smile. "Not today. How are your samples holding out?"

Sawyer shrugged. "Never saw a town so hard to convince. That reminds me." He signaled the fat bartender. "The big boss in?"

The man shook his head.

"Know where I can find him? I may have to leave town in the morning, and I want to cinch the order before I go."

The man hesitated, glancing sidewise at Croyner. But the railroad paymaster had seen someone across the room at the rear poker table. He muttered something Sawyer did not catch and went away from the bar, carrying his half-filled glass.

The bartender said out of the side of his mouth, "There are steps behind the building. Climb them and knock twice." He turned away to serve a customer at the far end of the bar.

Sawyer took time to finish his drink. He lighted a cigar and sauntered from the room, giving the appearance of a man who has no place to go and nothing on his mind. He paused outside to watch three riders come up the street at a run, almost slide their horses to the rack before him, and dismount with a deal of clowning.

"Last man in buys the first round."

They struggled at the doorway of the saloon, each claiming victory at the top of his lungs. Sawyer walked slowly to the corner. He glanced back casually. No one had followed him from the saloon.

He loafed along the side street to the mouth of the alley and stepped into its shadows. Moving swiftly now, he reached the rear of the saloon. There were lights in the rooms above, and he climbed the stairs and knocked on the door twice.

The door was pulled open sharply, and Jumbo Wilson stood facing him, holding a heavy gun. The man wore nothing but an undershirt, and it was obvious that he had been in bed.

"Oh, it's you. Come in, quick."

Sawyer stepped through the door. Jumbo shut it and swung

around. There was no friendship in his heavy voice. "You talk to Croyner?"

"Twice." Sawyer was as abrupt as the larger man.

"What'd you find out?"

"The pay car is coming through next week."

Jumbo snorted. "They been saying the same thing for the last thirty days."

"Look, you must have some connections in Spokane. How about letting me go there and find out?"

Suspicion made Jumbo's big face more repulsive than usual. "Why are you so all-fired anxious to get out of here? If Joel had wanted you in Spokane, he'd have sent you there. Get out, and don't come back until you get the dope from Croyner."

Sawyer said levelly, "I'm afraid that won't work. If you don't want me in Spokane, send me somewhere else. I can't stay here."

"Why?"

"The boss's sister just came in on the evening train."

Wilson jumped. "Virginia? In Milton? What in hell is she doing here?"

Sawyer shrugged. "Following me, according to her story." He went on to report everything the girl had said. "I made the slip of mentioning Joel. She's suspicious. She threatened to go to the sheriff and the railroad officials in the morning."

Wilson swore loudly. "I can't believe it."

Sawyer's shrug was more expressive than words. "I only know what she said. You know more about her than I do."

The big man started to pace the floor. He was finding it hard to make up his mind. Usually he left decisions to Joel Kelly. He planted himself in front of Sawyer.

"That dame. She's given Joel nothing but trouble ever since I've known him. Me, I'd break her neck, but no, he lets her go ahead and make trouble. What in hell good is it going to do for you to go to Spokane? She can still go to the sheriff and the railroad and tell them what she suspects."

"If I leave town maybe she won't suspect anything. Maybe she'll follow me like she said."

Wilson turned this over slowly in his mind. "How's she going to find out you're leaving?"

"I'll think of a way to let her know."

"Then she'll follow you there."

It was the last thing Sawyer wanted, having someone follow him to Spokane, but he saw no alternative. He merely shrugged.

"All right." Jumbo Wilson reluctantly made up his mind. "I guess there ain't no other way out. Joel won't like this, but what else are we going to do? There's a man in the Sailors' Bank named Al Tupper. Get in touch with him as soon as you get there. Tell him the moon is high over Montana."

Sawyer repressed a smile. It was like Joel Kelly to use such a flowery phrase as a password. He had begun to suspect that Kelly, despite his ruthlessness, was at heart a romanticist.

"Tupper will know when the pay car is due. Wire me." Wilson grinned slightly. "The name is Tiny Bowers."

Sawyer returned the grin.

"Give us as much notice as you can. A letter care of the saloon downstairs will reach me if there's time. Now blow."

Sawyer went back down the ladderlike stairs into the darkness of the alley and along it to the side street. The street was empty. He moved hurriedly to the hotel, noting by the lobby clock that it was twelve thirty-five.

There was a train west at three thirty.

He went directly to the deserted desk and turned the ledger that served as a register. Virginia Kelly was in Room Twelve.

He climbed the stairs. He went back along the upper hall and found that Twelve was the last door on the right. He paused, listening. No sound came from within. No thread of light showed through the large crack beneath the door.

He knocked. For a long minute there was no response, and he knocked again. This time her voice reached him, carrying an underlying note of panic.

"Who is it?"

"Sawyer."

Again there was silence, as if she was striving to get enough breath to speak. "Are you . . . drunk?"

He laughed. He could not help it. For some reason the laugh must have reassured her, for he heard her feet on the floor, heard her say, "A minute, please."

She struck a match and lighted a lamp. The door was ill-hung, ill-fitting, so that light showed not only at the bottom but along the sides where the panel did not quite meet the jamb. He heard the rustle as she slipped into a wrap. Then she pulled the bolt and was standing before him.

Her soft blond hair fell loosely about her shoulders. The light wrap was blue over the whiteness of a nightgown. The gown had a yoke of embroidery with blue flowers worked into it, the blue matching the deep color of her eyes. Her bare feet, peering from the bottom edge of the gown, were small, delicate, well-formed.

Sawyer caught his breath. It was involuntary. She was lovely, her eyes still shadowed from deep sleep. She was conscious of his reaction and a faint color came into the round of her cheeks, but her voice was steady and without embarrassment.

"What do you want?"

His tone was roughened by the emotion that surged through him. "I came to say good-by."

Her eyes mirrored her sharp surprise. "You're leaving Milton?"

"On the three-thirty train."

She was watching him, her manner wary now. "It seems a little strange, your coming to tell me."

He took his cue from his own emotion. "I simply wanted to see you again. I suspect this is the last time we'll meet."

Her manner again changed. "Sawyer, I told you you're a poor liar."

"Now what?"

"It doesn't make sense, your coming here, waking me, telling me you're leaving, when you know that I intend to hound you until I see you hanged."

He forced a laugh. "Men are not always logical when a pretty woman is involved."

She ignored this. She went on as if he had not spoken. "It doesn't make sense, unless you want me to follow you for reasons of your own."

"Anyone would want you to follow them."

She actually stamped one bare foot. "Stop it. You're no more clever with pretty speeches than you are with lies. You want me to follow. Why? Because something is going to happen in this town, something involving Joel. You were shocked when you first saw me tonight. You were worried. You aren't now. What's happened in the last hour? Have you seen Joel? Has he given you orders to get me out of town?"

"I have not seen Joel."

She studied his face. He had the sensation that she might even be able to read his mind. There was something uncanny about their relationship, as if they were bound together by some tie that neither of them understood.

"I think you're telling me the truth now." She said this slowly, as if not quite sure of her own reasoning. "Don't ask me why I think so. But something has happened, and you want me to follow you. Well, I'm not going to. I'm going to the sheriff in the morning and tell him that Joel is planning something in Milton. After that I'll pick up your trail again. Good night."

Before he could answer the door had closed, and he found himself facing the dark panel.

He stood motionless, knowing he should be relieved. He did not want the girl to trail him to Spokane. Her presence there would complicate things and make his job more difficult. But there was something else to worry about. She could go to Croyner and the sheriff and drop her warning. The name Joel Kelly carried a sinister ring, and there were nearly a dozen separate rewards on the bandit's head. Any peace officer west of Omaha would not ignore even the most uncertain tip that might lead to Kelly's capture.

He turned and went to his own room, where he packed swiftly. On the way to the station he left a note with the fat bartender of the Bitterroot, telling him to get it to Wilson at once. The note merely said that Virginia Kelly had refused the bait, that she was remaining in Milton, and that she meant to talk to both the sheriff and Croyner in the morning. The rest was up to Wilson.

Chapter Six

MARC SAWYER reached the Milton station fifteen minutes before train time. He was carrying his two sample cases and his personal grip.

They were heavy, and he felt that they were stretching his arms a good three inches. He came around the corner of the weathered building and stopped.

Virginia Kelly sat perched on a baggage truck in the full beam of lamplight thrown from the station's bay. He stood gaping, then slowly moved forward to the edge of the truck and set down his grips.

His first thought was that no one could look so fresh and dainty at this hour of the morning. He himself felt grimy and dirty. He was unshaven, and his tired clothes were rumpled.

She said, "Surprised?" with no friendliness in her voice.

He told her, "It's been a long time since anything a woman does has surprised me."

She slid off the truck and faced him. Even in this motion she was graceful, and he wished deeply that they had met under other circumstances.

Never before had the thought of marriage crossed his mind, He had resigned himself to the fact that a man in his occupation should have no permanent ties, that his life would be spent crossing and recrossing the dim trails left by outlaws as they slipped quietly through the hills.

But for a woman this life . . . He checked himself. She was Joel Kelly's sister. He could not trust her.

"Marc Sawyer"—she said his name deliberately—"I told you I would hound you until the day you hang. I meant it. I'm also going to keep you worrying and guessing. Just when you think you know what I'll do next, I'll do something else. That's why I changed my mind. That's why I'm following you tonight."

He was spared the necessity of answering by the whistle of the approaching train. He turned without a word and went into the station. He stepped across the dirty, splintered floor and bought a ticket to Spokane. As he swung away she moved to the counter.

"A ticket to Spokane, please."

He wondered what Jumbo Wilson would think when he found her gone. It would give the big man something fresh to worry about. Sawyer did not care. Having the girl in Spokane would bring him complications of his own; there was no need to fret over Wilson's problems.

The train carried three coaches and no sleeping car. The forward coach was the smoker, and Sawyer turned into it. He was tempted to trail the girl into the middle car, but resisted the impulse. It would be pleasant to have her company on the long ride, but he no longer trusted himself in her presence. Besides, he meant to shake her before the train got to Spokane.

He could do this easily. From long familiarity with the railroads he knew that the train would slow down when it reached the edge of the sprawling yards, that it might even stop so the brakeman could drop off to throw the switch and give them a clear track to the station.

All the monotonous day as they wound through the badlands of upper Idaho and into the dry stretches of western Washington, he drowsed on the cindery seat. He had learned to take what rest he could. At each station stop he dropped down to the platform, and each time he saw Virginia Kelly also leave her car and watch him, making sure that he did not duck away from the train. He grinned. Only at the eating stops, where they were crowded into fly-infested dining rooms, did he acknowledge her presence by even a nod.

Of one thing he was certain. She would not invade the smoking car. This was a male preserve, and no woman would think of sticking her nose into the ill-ventilated sanctuary.

He dozed after the last stop, knowing they still had a seventy-five-mile run. The grip of the brakes, slowing the train at the border of the yards, roused him.

He caught up the heavy cases, tempted to leave them. Under his breath he swore that no matter what happened to him he would never be a traveling salesman.

He opened the car's forward door and stepped out onto the wind-ridden platform. Before him the rear of the tender rose like a black gate. Smoke beat around him from the wheezing engine; hot sparks burned his face.

He eased down the open steps, feeling the pull of the train's brakes, seeing the wink of the signal lamps in the gray overcast of the early dawn, gauging his moment. He swung down just as the train lost momentum, as the engineer pulled on the dragbar to decrease his speed.

Sawyer held his footing despite the swing of the heavy bags. He had a moment for wry humor, thinking of the whiskey that would be spilled if he caught his foot in one of the switch frogs. Then he regained his balance and stood, breathing heavily, watching the train glide by, wondering if the girl had seen him beside the track in the semidarkness.

He watched the green and red tail lanterns ease to a halt beside the distant station, then moved quickly and surely across the yards toward the long wooden building that housed the division offices.

He climbed the stairs and went into Paul Chum's office. He lit the green-shaded student's lamp above the desk, then summoned a boy and sent him scurrying to Chum's boarding-house. Next he sat down in the chair before the desk and did something he had seldom done in his eventful life. He drew a bottle from one of his sample cases and had a drink by himself.

Afterward, with a cigar burning between his lips, he gazed unseeing at the far wall, at the map that diagramed the railway system in careful detail, and weighed his situation.

The West, which to most people was a land of boundless distances, was to him a familiar street. He had traveled it with the regularity with which most men traveled between their business and their home. He had used trains, stages, horses, and even mules. He had poked into remote hideouts where no men except the members of the gangs had ever been.

That he was alive was a matter of luck or, as he preferred to think, good sense. But he knew that luck ran out and that reckoning might always wait across the next mountain. His body bore the scars of half a dozen gunshot wounds, and each time he set out on a new trail he knew that it might well be the last.

Noise on the stairs brought him out of the desk chair, and he was standing when Paul Chum hurried through the doorway.

Chum was a gray man in a pepper-and-salt suit. The gray was not from age but from long and excessive work. His hair, which had been blond in youth, had grayed as a badger's coat grays, his skin had a tinge of unhealthy gray under the tan, and his lips lacked color of any kind. It might have been the face of a dead man.

But when he smiled his eyes gained lights and his face came alive, revealing that the grayness came from overwork, from worry, from long hours spent trying to keep the new railroad above the surface of the sea of debt that threatened to engulf it.

"Marc."

Sawyer grinned. Chum was a cautious man. Even in the shelter of his own office, at this early hour when the building held only a skeleton crew, he would not take the chance of using Sawyer's real name.

"Where'd you come from?"

Marc told him in a hundred graphic words. He was used to making cryptic reports, sometimes in a double-talk as confusing as any code. He wasted neither time nor breath.

"We've got him." He seldom allowed himself enthusiasm, but the chase of Joel Kelly had been a long one and nearly every railroad agent in the West had had his chance at it.

Chum sat down at his desk. "You sure?"

Sawyer told him exactly what had happened, even repeating some of the short reports he had sent in to clarify the picture.

"They framed me for Pierson's death, so they're sure of me. They didn't need me on this particular job. They could have found out when the pay car was coming through. They're giving me a test before they turn me loose on a whole string of jobs. But this shipment is too big to let them get away with. This will be their last job."

Chum sighed heavily. He had a high regard for both Sawyer's ability and his judgment, but it seemed almost too much to believe that this would be the last of Joel Kelly. Not since the James boys had cut their swath across the deep Middle West, directly after the war, had any group of outlaws given the railroads and the banks as much trouble.

"I hope you're right. This is the biggest gold shipment we've ever sent into Milton, and it's got to get through, Kelly or no Kelly. How do you want to work it?"

Sawyer said, "I'm supposed to contact a man named Tupper at the Sailors' Bank. He's to find out for me when the car will be sent."

Chum started. "Tupper? I don't believe it. Why, I've known him five years. He's the bank's cashier. He helped start it."

Sawyer shrugged. His work had made him cynical; he suspected almost everyone until he was proved innocent.

"That's the word. I wouldn't be surprised if Kelly's connections reach a lot higher places than Tupper. The man is a born organizer. If he'd gone in a different direction, he might well be president of the railroad."

Chum's smile was sour. "He might yet. He must be piling

up a fortune. We've had men checking the foreign banks. We know he has a lot of money hidden somewhere, but we haven't been able to locate it." He brooded for a moment.

"Well, what do you want me to do?"

Sawyer told him, "Put the pay car between two baggage cars. Have half a dozen men in each and six more in the coach. There's a grade about three miles west of Milton. The train slows down there until it's barely crawling. I'll arrange to have Kelly hit it there, and we'll be waiting for him."

"What about warning the local authorities?"

Sawyer shook his head. "We can't take the chance. A whisper that anything is up and Kelly would be five hundred miles away."

"Any preference as to who I send?"

"Bob Holt if he's around. I want someone with a level head to handle the men. I don't want anyone except Holt to know who I am. If we miss for any reason, I want to hold my cover."

Chum nodded.

"There's one more thing. Kelly's sister, the one who was married to Pierson, is in Spokane. She came in on the train with me."

Chum whistled. "Following you?"

Sawyer shrugged and told him about the girl. "I can't make up my mind whether or not she's serious about trying to hound me because of her husband's death. Kelly's clever as a cornered fox. It may be that he's using her as a plant to keep testing me, to keep track of what I'm doing."

"But maybe she did love her husband. Maybe she is trying to avenge his death."

"And maybe she merely married him at her brother's orders, to smoke out the fact he was a railroad agent. It adds up that way. She came to Whitewater to see her brother about something important. It may have been to tell him that their suspicions were true, that Pierson was working for the Texas railroad and that he had to die."

Chum's smile was sardonic. "I'd hate to live with so suspicious a mind."

"You live longer that way." Sawyer stood up. "I'll be at the Fenton Hotel. Which day does the car go?"

"Wednesday, on the midnight train. That would put it into Milton about two in the morning. I judge you'd rather have it at night."

"Probably better. It won't make much difference if it's clear. The moon will be full. I'll contact Tupper. I have to make it look right. Besides, we'll want to know as much about him as we can when the showdown comes."

He left the building and crossed the yard to the station platform, still carrying his heavy grips. He had no idea where Virginia Kelly was staying and at the moment he did not care. He had seen Chum and was certain that no one aside from the call boy knew of his meeting with the division superintendent. It was full daylight by the time he got a hack and was driven up the raw streets to the hotel. He got his room, sponged the dirt of the journey from his body, and changed into clean clothes.

He looked hungrily at the bed, but this was not a time for sleep. When this chase was over he meant to spend a full two weeks in bed.

He was eating breakfast in the restaurant across from the hotel when someone paused beside his table, and he glanced up to see Virginia Kelly. She looked as fresh as usual. Again he wondered how she did it.

"So you thought you could give me the slip?"

He grinned up at her, suddenly enjoying himself. "If I had known where you were staying, I would have invited you to breakfast. I hate to eat alone."

She sat down. "You're lying, as usual. How'd you manage to get off the train without my seeing you?"

His grin widened. "An old trick. Trains have two sides."

Contempt came into her voice. "I can understand lies when they serve some purpose but not when they are told unnecessarily. Don't you think I have sense enough to look under a train to see if someone is dropping off on the far side?"

He told her the truth then, but not the full truth. "I dropped off when the train slowed down for the yard limits. I thought it would give you something to chew on."

"You'd go a long way to worry me, like carrying those heavy bags clear up to the station to get a hack."

He stared at her, and it was her turn to smile. "Oh, I was inside the baggage room. I told the agent I felt faint, that I wanted to rest before going on up to the hotel."

"And you followed me to the hotel?"

"I followed you."

He was laughing now. "I underestimated you. You're good."

She watched him, not knowing quite how to take this. The waitress came, and she ordered. Then she leaned forward, resting her elbows on the table, her chin in her hands.

"Sawyer, I don't understand you yet. I haven't from the first. You aren't stupid. You've had education somewhere. Why . . . why does a man like you fall in with my brother?"

"I told you. Money."

"What if I were to offer you money, more money than you'll ever get out of Joel?"

He was genuinely startled.

"Surprises you?"

"It does."

"I've been thinking things over. You're the man who shot Floyd and I should hate you, but somehow I don't. I don't quite understand why, but maybe it's because, better than anyone else, I realize the tremendous power Joel exerts over people. He's made me do many things in my life that I'm heartily ashamed of. It wasn't until I married Floyd that I found the strength to break away."

Sawyer did not answer. Her breakfast came, but she only picked listlessly at the eggs and fried sidemeat.

"You don't believe me?"

"I didn't say that."

"I'll never forgive you for killing Floyd. No woman ever

could. But I'll stop bothering you if you'll help me. I'll pay you everything I have."

"Help you how?"

"To get Joel. To stop him from committing any further crimes."

"To stop him? How? Kill him?" Sawyer's voice was blunt.

He saw the horror shade down across her eyes. Her voice was faint. "Why do men always think first about killing?"

He said sharply, "There are only two ways to stop a man like Joel Kelly. Kill him or send him to prison. And sending Joel to prison, from what I've heard, is not the easiest thing in the world. Everyone knows that he's responsible for a lot of holdups. They are certain he has had people murdered. But can they prove it?"

She said, "You don't sound as if you'd be against having it done."

He caught himself, realizing that he had almost slipped into a trap. This woman was certainly dangerous for him.

He said flatly, "Shall I put it this way? I play things by percentages. Frankly I don't believe you stand a chance of tripping Joel. Frankly I think my chances are better to string along with him."

She withdrew into herself. All the sparkle that had animated her face during the last few minutes vanished, leaving her cold, distant.

"I had hoped for better than that."

He shoved back his chair, glancing at his watch. "I have to go to the bank. I'll see you later."

"That you will." Her tone was grim. "Since you won't help me, I'll try to nail you when I nail Joel."

"I could warn your brother." He was on his feet.

"You needn't bother. I've warned him enough. Joel just laughs."

Sawyer turned away, conscious that she was watching him through the restaurant window as he crossed the dusty street and angled toward the Sailors' Bank.

He came into the long room with its plain wooden counters, its huge safe. He stopped before the first clerk, asked for

Mr. Tupper, and was motioned toward the rear, where two private offices were partitioned off from the main room by low board fences. The door of the first was marked CASHIER, and he knocked, and at the invitation of the man within, opened the door.

Tupper was nearing forty. His hair was thin and sandy, his eyes blue and watery, and his chin came down to almost a point under the narrow slackness of a weak mouth.

His coat hung neatly from a tree in the corner, and the sleeves of his ruffled shirt were protected by sateen slip-ons.

He looked up, peering at Sawyer through square-lensed, steel-framed glasses.

"Yes?"

Sawyer said, loudly enough to be heard by the clerks in the outer room, "I represent the Old Reliable Distillery of York, Pennsylvania. I have a draft on the Drovers' Bank of Philadelphia, which I would appreciate your honoring."

He sat down at the man's desk, producing the draft. "I have been covering the West pretty thoroughly, and I find it interesting, especially when the moon is high over Montana."

He caught the flicker of surprise in the watery eyes. The man behind the desk sat motionless, as if he could not make up his mind.

"What part of Montana were you in, friend?"

"I came in from Milton on this morning's train."

"I see. I understand that the spur the Montana Central is building south is coming along nicely."

"Everything except that the men have not been paid. I wonder when the pay car is finally going out."

The man made up his mind. "Joel sent you."

"Wilson."

"You're the whiskey drummer I heard about?"

"I guess so."

"I don't know yet when the pay car leaves, but as soon as I learn I'll let you know. What hotel are you staying at?"

Sawyer told him in a low tone, and Tupper raised his voice. "As soon as I can clear it I'll send word to your hotel."

Chapter Seven

THE train was mixed; a boxcar behind the engine, a baggage car, the pay car, another baggage car, a smoker, and a single day coach.

None of the excitement Sawyer felt showed in the smooth contour of his face as he stood on the platform waiting for the train to start. There were a dozen armed men in the two baggage cars, and Bob Holt had six more with him in the smoker.

Sawyer had no idea how many riders would be with Kelly in the holdup, but he doubted that the bandit leader would use too many.

He paced the platform, reviewing each step he had taken, trying to find a weak spot in his plans.

Tupper had gotten in touch with him at noon of the first day with the information that the pay car would go out on the Wednesday midnight train. The identity of Tupper's contact with the railroad had not yet been learned, but the banker was under close surveillance.

Sawyer's careful note to Wilson setting the details of the holdup had been handed to the mail clerk on the first eastbound train, and should already be in the big man's hands. Where Kelly and the gang were hiding, Sawyer did not know, but they could not be far from Milton.

Someone spoke his name, and he wheeled to find Viriginia Kelly behind him.

"So you still think you can slip away from me."

He stared at her. They had not spoken to each other in the last three days, although he had seen her several times on the street. In a town so small it would have been difficult not to run into each other.

"You're going back to Milton." It was an accusation, not a question.

He did not deny it.

"I should warn you. I talked to the division superintendent. I told him that you and Joel were planning something."

He had a sudden vision of Chum listening to her recital. Not daring to contact the man after the first morning, he had made all his arrangements through Bob Holt.

"I hope he listened to you." He was trying desperately to think of a way to keep her from boarding the train. How she had discovered his impending departure was something he could not imagine.

He had slipped from the hotel's rear door without checking out, without taking his baggage.

"I don't know. He thanked me, that's all."

Sawyer wished he dared believe her. He wished he had time to check her statement with Chum. If what she had told him now was true, it meant that she had been on the level all along, that she actually was out to stop her brother.

The conductor's voice echoed along the platform.

"All aboard."

His lantern came up, then down, in the highball, and the train began to move.

Sawyer had to be on that train, but he tried to wait until it was moving too swiftly for the girl to swing aboard. Again she seemed to read his mind. Without waiting for him, she ran across the platform and with the conductor's help, lifted herself up the steps of the day coach.

Sawyer had no choice but to follow. He caught the handrail and swung himself up, and the conductor, who did not know who he was, reproved him.

"That's a good way to get yourself killed."

He said, "I guess you're right," and went on into the

coach. From force of habit he examined the passengers with a long, sweeping glance.

The car was better than half-filled. Four riders, their saddles stacked in the aisle, had already started a poker game in the end seats, a slicker stretched across their knees to serve as a table.

There were half a dozen drummers and four women. Two of the women sat together. The third was old, a shawl about her hunched shoulders.

Virginia Kelly sat alone, halfway back, and Sawyer noticed that already every salesman in the car was trying, unsuccessfully, to catch her eye.

He smiled wryly to himself and moved down the swaying aisle. The train began picking up speed as it cleared the limits of the yard. He stopped beside her seat and said in a low voice, "May I sit down?"

She answered with a slight nod, and he folded himself onto the cinder-scarred cushion at her side. They rode in silence for a good two miles, the lights of the town falling behind them until only the distant moon lighted the rolling land.

She asked then, "Is Joel going to hold up this train?"

He turned his head. "What makes you think that?"

"When I was at the railroad office this evening I heard that this train was carrying the pay car."

He repressed his start. He had not expected the division office would be so careless.

"I think I'll speak to the conductor. He can wire ahead from the next station, can't he?"

Sawyer shrugged. He wished the next thirty hours were over. If she continued to push, she could well spoil all his plans. He said, "Speak to the conductor if you want to." He rose then and left her, going forward into the smoker.

Bob Holt sat by himself in one of the rear seats, his men strung along the car among the regular passengers. In their nondescript clothes they looked no different from any other travelers.

Sawyer paused beside Holt. "This seat taken?"

Bob Holt looked up indifferently. He was a slender man of medium height, with auburn hair that grew down to sideburns framing his face.

"Help yourself."

Sawyer sat down. Holt was a good operative, cool-headed in emergencies. Sawyer had worked with him before. The man dressed like a gambler and had, in fact, dealt faro in a Denver saloon before joining the railroad.

There was a man, apparently asleep, in the seat ahead of them. Sawyer turned to face Holt, lowering his voice so that the creaking grind of the train buried his words, his mouth forming each word slowly so that Holt was almost able to read his lips.

"Wire Chum from the next station. Tell our conductor to hold the train until you get an answer. Find out if Virginia Kelly talked to Chum tonight, if she warned him her brother and I were going to try a holdup."

Holt nodded. He asked no questions. That was one of the things Sawyer liked about him. Sawyer lit a cigar and leaned back, closing his eyes. The train moved on, cutting its noisy way through the quiet of the night, the glow from its stack lighting the rolling hills on either side.

It was morning before they reached Carson. The station was a boxlike building whose yellow paint had already begun to dull. They came to their grinding stop so that the smoker's open rear door was directly opposite the station bay.

Sawyer moved leisurely down the three steps to the splintered boards. He turned and saw Holt drop from the front end of the car and walk to where the agent stood talking to the conductor and the engineer. A minute later Holt and the agent moved toward the station.

Virginia Kelly descended the steps of the day coach. She met Sawyer's eyes steadily, then hurried toward the conductor, now advancing back along the train.

She talked to him vehemently; then they, too, went into the station.

Sawyer tossed his cigar into the ditch between the platform edge and the train, and climbed again into the smoker. Holt joined him half an hour later as the train began to move, and Sawyer spoke without opening his eyes.

"Well?"

"She talked to Chum, all right, but she didn't mention her brother. It was all about you and how you were planning something dangerous for the railroad."

Sawyer thought this over. "When she went into the station with the conductor, what did she want?"

"Wanted him to wire Chum for authority to put you off the train."

"Nothing about her brother?"

"Not a word."

Sawyer knew a deep sense of regret. He had so nearly convinced himself that she had been honest with him.

"Wonder what she thinks she's up to?" Holt was speaking.

"Probably some scheme of Kelly's. Make certain she sends no more wires from the stops ahead. Tell the agents to accept them but to sit on them. Joel is pulling a switch."

"Meaning you think he won't hold up the train?"

"I don't know. I wish I did." Sawyer rose and headed back to the coach.

Virginia Kelly was in the same seat, curled up like a kitten, apparently asleep. He sat down across the aisle from her, leaned against the dirty window, pulled his hat low over his eyes to shade them from the glow of the swinging lamps, and let the motion of the train rock him into a fitful sleep.

When he woke the train was motionless. Outside, it was still daylight. The girl's seat was empty.

He stared at it stupidly, then swung around and raised the blind to peer through the dirt-streaked glass.

He was in time to see her come from the station building, followed a few seconds later by Holt. Sawyer rose and with deceptive casualness, swiftly traversed the aisle and crossed over the bridging platform to the sanctuary of the smoker. When the train was again in motion, Holt appeared and dropped into the seat at his side.

"What did she try to send this time?"

Holt gave him a small grin. "She addressed a wire to a Jumbo Wilson. It read, 'Deal off. Explain later,' and she signed your name to it."

Sawyer swore under his breath. "The agent didn't send it?"

"The agent did not send it."

They rode in silence. Neither had anything to say.

Chapter Eight

BY THE TIME the train was within forty miles of Milton it was deep night, and the tension within the smoker had mounted until even Bob Holt, who normally seemed to lack nerves of any kind, was taut and jumpy.

He fidgeted. He went into the baggage car ahead and checked the six men there. He checked the two guards in the pay car and the men in the forward baggage car.

He rejoined Sawyer in the smoker, and sank heavily into his seat, mopping his face.

"I guess we're set."

"The main thing," Sawyer told him, "is to get Kelly and Wilson, and a man named Kirk, a redhead. I'd like them all, but the rest don't really matter."

"You sure they'll hit us on the grade?"

Sawyer's shrug was expressive. "I'm not sure of anything. That's what I told Wilson, but Kelly may have other plans. All we can do is try to be ready to meet anything. If we fail this time, we probably won't get another chance. At least my usefulness on this one will be gone."

"I've put one man up in the cab. They'll likely use a couple of riders to flag the engine down. The fireman is also armed."

"All right." Sawyer rose. "I'll keep an eye on the girl. I don't know whether or not there's a gun in her bag, but I wouldn't be too surprised. I suspect she's capable of nearly everything."

Most of the regular smoker passengers were sleeping. He stepped onto the apron between cars and stood for a minute, filling his lungs with the windy air, listening to the click of wheels against rail joints, to the steady *chuff* of the engine, wincing at the swirl of hot cinders that bit his face.

From all appearances Virginia Kelly was asleep. He sat down in the seat opposite her and studied her face. It was relaxed, childlike in repose, and in spite of himself a tenderness welled up inside him.

Hers could not have been an easy life, even if she had utterly approved everything her brother had done. Unconsciously he searched her features for signs of viciousness, and found none. Whatever her experiences had been, they had not marked her externally. He wished he could look into her mind the way she at times seemed able to look into his.

He turned his head and peered from the sooted window, trying to determine exactly where they were.

Outside, the moon was a full disk in the milky sky, and the brush and rock appeared grotesque, distorted by deep shadows, as if some master painter had dipped his brush into blacks and spread them boldly across the world.

The train checked its speed. They must have reached the grade, Sawyer thought, and he glanced quickly at his watch. But according to the timetable they should not be there for another twenty minutes.

The train slowed jerkily, as if the brakes had been applied suddenly, and Sawyer left his seat swiftly, like a well-coordinated cat. He reached the heavy door and dragged it open.

There was no question about it, the train was stopping. Sawyer swung down the steps, and grabbing the handrails, leaned out as far as he could. The train was well into a curve perhaps a mile long, the track arcing so that he had a full view ahead. In the distance half a dozen red lanterns formed a necklace across the track.

He felt a surge as the engine man eased the bar and the train began to pick up a portion of its lost momentum.

A man was leaning from the front steps of the smoker, and Sawyer realized that it was Bob Holt.

They were now traveling at some ten miles an hour, as if the engineer could not make up his mind about the lights ahead, as if he held only enough speed on the train to keep it moving.

And then as the straightening track blotted out Sawyer's view and he could no longer see the warning lights, the power was cut and the train drifted to a halt, stopped by a slight upgrade.

Before motion ceased, Sawyer dropped to the rough, uncertain footing of the right of way.

He ran toward Bob Holt and called his question, and got nothing but a shrug in return. The conductor, who had apparently been asleep in the smoker, came chuffing after them, a tall, nervous man with a long, underslung jaw.

They ran toward the engine together. As they passed the baggage cars, the side doors slid back and Holt's men crowded the openings. Holt called to them to stay where they were.

The engineer, the fireman, and the guard were down out of the cab by the time they reached the front of the train, and they went forward in a group to examine the row of red lights spaced across the track. Yet when they got there it was not the lights that held their attention. It was the bridge beyond—or rather the place where the bridge had been.

The span was gone. Its only remnant was a few splintered ties held crookedly by the spikes still binding them to the twisted rails. Dynamite had torn out the heavy stringers that had bridged the wash, leaving a gap more than twenty-five feet wide.

Holt turned to Sawyer, his grin wry, his tone thin and angry. "Looks like your friend has ideas of his own when it comes to stopping a train. I'd better warn the men. I'm surprised we haven't been attacked already." He turned and trotted back, Sawyer at his side.

Suddenly he stopped, pointing. On the curve they had

rounded only minutes before, a dozen lights jittered and danced.

"They're tearing up the track so we can't back up. What do we do now, Mr. Sawyer?"

Sawyer watched the lights. There was not much they could do now. Kelly had built his trap nicely. Now the train could not move either way. There was no help closer than Milton, still thirty miles east. He glanced up at the telegraph wire sagging between the poles that paralleled the right of way.

Holt saw the look. "Probably cut. Kelly would think of the wire first."

"There are some climbers in the baggage car. Try it. If you can get a message through, fine. We may be able to hold them off. But Kelly's no fool, and we're like a sitting duck. How many rifles do we have?"

"Only a dozen. I figured they'd board the moving train on the grade and we'd take them by surprise. If the guards had brought rifles into the coach, it would have been a tip-off, and the conductor is the only member of the crew I trust. That's the hell of fighting Kelly, you don't know who is in his pay."

They were interrupted by a shout from the brush to the left. "Hello, the train."

Sawyer would have recognized that voice anywhere. There was no mistaking Jumbo's raucous bray.

His hand tightened on Holt's arm warningly. "That's Wilson." He spoke in an undertone.

"Hello, the train. Can you hear me, Mr. Conductor?"

Holt growled, "Anybody'd have to be dead not to hear that bellow. I'd like a straight shot at him."

From beside the engine the conductor had turned. "I hear you. What do you want?"

"Then hear me good. The roadbed under you is planted with dynamite. You've got exactly three minutes to fetch everyone off that train. Everyone. Do you understand?"

There was a silence as the conductor tried to realize what the words meant. Holt's tone was low. "Think that's the truth?"

Sawyer's voice was tight. "With Kelly, nothing in the world surprises me. And it doesn't matter if it's the truth or not. We can't move the train, and I can't risk having a hundred people killed in an explosion."

Wilson's shout came again. "Do you understand? Tell them to march off, and if any of them have guns, they're to leave them in the train. We've got twenty men out here watching. Your first shot and we'll cut you to pieces."

Holt was swearing in a dull monotone. "Get the passengers off. Leave my guards. We'll take care of the bastards."

Sawyer had a vision of the train being blown up. He shook his head. "Tell the conductor to get everyone off, and don't try anything funny. Don't forget, the engine and cars are worth more than fifty thousand."

This was something Holt had not considered, and angry as he was, he was gambler enough to throw in an unplayable hand.

"So he beat us."

"Maybe, maybe not. Take your crew and the passengers far enough from the train to be out of harm's way. Remember, Kelly's men have horses. They can ride you down if they choose to. As soon as you have the chance, climb a pole and try to reach Milton. If you can't raise them, get there as fast as you can and turn the country out. I'll try to leave you some kind of a trail to follow."

"You're going with them?"

"If they'll take me, and they'll take me if they don't suspect I've got any connection with you. Get moving."

He watched Holt run forward to the conductor's side. The two men argued, then both turned and ran along the train, Holt to get his guards from the baggage and pay cars, the conductor to clear the coach and smoker.

Sawyer stayed in the shadow of the train. The ground at the right of way was low enough so that his head was below the level of the lighted windows. He scanned the rough floor of the valley through which the track ran. Beyond, showing mysterious and silver in the moonlight, the hills climbed toward higher peaks. Some of that land beyond the valley's lips was as rough and impassable as any within the United States. Somewhere in those mountains Kelly undoubtedly had a hideout. Somewhere in those mountains he would feel safe from pursuit. Then they would see.

The sleepy, bewildered passengers were already stringing down the train's steps, herded by the conductor like a worried hen with too many chicks.

One of the last was Virginia Kelly. Sawyer stared at her. In the excitement he had completely forgotten that she was on the train.

He could let her go with the rest, but if he did she was bound to learn from the talk of some of Holt's men that there had been a guard on the train. He moved swiftly and had her arm before she realized what he was about.

"This way. The roadbed is mined." He led her quickly forward, away from the other passengers, who were already half-screened by the waist-high brush.

"Hello, the train." It was Wilson again. "Sawyer, are you there?"

With a convulsive jerk the girl tried to pull free, but Sawyer's fingers bit into her arm.

"Let me go." There was a desperate note in her voice.

He held his grip. He watched the big figure of Wilson loom out of the night, curbing his nervous horse only when he reached Sawyer's side.

"Who's that?" He was looking at the struggling girl.

"Kelly's sister."

"Well, I'll be damned. What's she doing here?"

"Following me, as usual."

"All the passengers off the train?"

"Right."

"Half a dozen of the boys are hazing them back through the brush, just in case." He put a thick thumb and forefinger into his mouth, and his whistle would have done credit to a locomotive.

They rode in from three directions, circling. Sawyer counted twelve, and they came well-mounted, well-ordered, approaching the train gingerly. A couple of men swung out of their saddles to run up the car steps, making certain the train was empty.

Sawyer's respect for Joel Kelly, already high, rose again. Kelly rode to where they stood. In the light from the coach windows, his hazel eyes glowed like a cat's and his tight-lipped smile showed the satisfaction of a supreme egoist at a perfect accomplishment.

"Everything all right?"

"Fine," said Sawyer. "No problem."

"Hope you're not mad that we blew the bridge instead of stopping you on the grade." Kelly had expressed no surprise at seeing his sister. He spoke to Sawyer as if she were not present.

Sawyer managed a grin. "Why should I mind? There's fifty thousand in the pay car."

With a violent gesture Virginia Kelly broke free. She walked to her brother's side and stood looking up at him. Sawyer made no effort to stop her.

"Joel, I told you that if you pulled another holdup I'd turn you in."

Kelly grinned faintly. He stepped from the saddle as effortlessly as if he were taking a step on level ground. He stood, still smiling at her.

"You never learn, do you, Ginny?" He slapped her then, and Sawyer saw her head jerk back and could almost feel the force of the blow. Kelly slapped her again, hard, without passion, perfunctorily, as though performing a routine, necessary task.

"Get her baggage, Sawyer."

"I'm not going with you," she said. "I'm never going anywhere with you again."

Joel Kelly turned his head. "Kirk, put her on a horse and keep her there if you have to tie her in the saddle. Get the bags, Sawyer."

Marc Sawyer had no choice. He climbed into the coach for her luggage. When he reappeared, the redhead, Kirk, had the girl on a horse and was standing close guard. Sawyer took the bags, tied a lead rope through their handles, and slung them over his own horse.

Kelly, Wilson, and half a dozen outlaws had already moved along the train to where the pay car stood, its sliding doors standing open invitingly.

Jumbo Wilson was inside drilling the safe. Sawyer learned later that, he was an expert box man, that he had twice done time for burglary before he joined Kelly.

The explosion was a dull jolt in the vastness of the night, deadened by the sacks Wilson had piled around the safe door.

Kelly was the first into the smoke-filled car, and Sawyer followed him.

The door sagged, still held by one twisted hinge, but the lock had been blown clear off. Wilson was indeed an artist, and Sawyer glanced at him with new interest. In his time he had seen some hundred safes that had been blown open. Most operators used too much powder. Often they destroyed or scattered much of the safe's contents. But here the neatly piled bags bearing the stamp of the Sailors' Bank had hardly shifted position.

Kelly reached in and hefted one of the sacks, hearing the clink as he tossed it in an arc through the air to Sawyer.

"This is the part I like." His eyes glowed. There was an eerie quality about him now. He seemed not quite human.

Sawyer realized suddenly that Kelly was money mad. His urge was not that of a normal man, desiring money for what it would buy. He wanted money for the possession of the money itself. Sawyer watched him curiously. Kelly was one of the most complex people he had ever met. It was no wonder that he broke all the rules of acceptable behavior, that he ignored the laws that bound ordinary men.

"Open it up. Let's look at it."

The mouth of the canvas bag was closed by a leather thong laced through tiny slits in the thick cloth. Sawyer knelt to unfasten the knot. He turned the bag and poured the coins onto the splintered floor.

A flood of metal washers made a small pile at his feet. He stared at them, stupefied. His first reaction was of utter disbelief. His second was of mounting rage, rage at Paul Chum. The division superintendent in trying to protect the company money had ruined everything. Whatever trust Kelly had had in him was probably wiped out.

He looked up into Kelly's blazing eyes. The man was hardly sane. He turned to the still-hot safe, snatched up a second sack, and practically tore the thong from its mouth. Another pile of washers spilled onto the floor around him. Then he took a quick step forward and before Sawyer guessed his intent, drove his fist directly into Sawyer's face.

The blow caught the angle of his jaw and dropped him to his knees without putting him entirely out. His whole impulse was to rise, to take Kelly apart, but as he came up Jumbo Wilson seized him from behind, throwing a soiled arm around his neck, and pulled his head backward until it seemed that his neck must break.

"Easy."

He stopped struggling. His head felt light, as though the top third were separated from the rest of his skull by an inch-deep cushion of air.

Blood leaked from a corner of his mouth, where one of his teeth had scraped the inside of his cheek. He spat on the floor in an effort to clear his breathing, and managed to say in a fairly normal voice, "It's all right. Let me go."

Wilson released his grip. Joel Kelly had already swung back to the safe and was methodically pulling out and emptying one bag after another. All were filled with washers. There was not a coin in any of them.

He turned slowly. All the rage that had shaken him during the first few moments of discovery had washed away, leaving him stunned.

"Suckered." His voice was bitter. "Suckered by the god-damn railroad." He stared at Sawyer with eyes that had lost their life. "What are you doing, working for them?"

Sawyer straightened his coat. He wiped his mouth with the back of his hand, leaving a smear of blood across the brown skin.

"That's not even funny. Would I be standing here now if I'd known what was going on?"

Kelly was not convinced; suspicion oozed from him. But he was slowly recovering from the shock of his disappointment.

"It's a trap. You probably had men planted on that grade where you expected us to hit the train. We caught you off guard by blowing the bridge."

Sawyer's agile mind was also recovering. "If it was a railroad trap, wouldn't there have been a lot of guards on the train? Use your head, Joel. I took Tupper's word for the time of shipment. I watched those money sacks being hauled from Tupper's bank and loaded into this car. You think it's a railroad trap? I've got another idea. How much do you know about Al Tupper?"

Kelly's eyes widened. "What are you talking about now?"

"Look at it from Tupper's angle." Sawyer was suddenly convinced that he was telling the actual truth. Paul Chum was too bright a man to substitute washers for the payroll. The railroad would chance any amount of money to catch Kelly.

"We know he isn't honest, or he wouldn't be giving you information. He knew this train was to be held up. So what was to prevent him from substituting washers for the gold and pocketing the money himself? After the holdup who would know? You would, but he wasn't afraid of you. You couldn't very well go to the railroad and say, 'Tupper is a crook. Tupper stole your money, I didn't.' "

Kelly blinked. Jumbo Wilson swore savagely. "He's right, Joel. I never did trust that Tupper. The bastard. I'll kill him the first chance I get."

"If you find him," Sawyer said. "He's probably already headed for Seattle, trying to get a ship out for the Orient. With that kind of money he could live like a prince out there for the rest of his life."

"I'll find him." Kelly was suddenly convinced. "I'll find him no matter where he tries to hide. And when I do I'll cut out his heart and eat it in front of him."

Sawyer shivered. He had heard many men make extravagant threats, but Kelly meant exactly what he said. The man had a deep streak of sadism. He was a brilliant yet unbalanced personality.

Kelly swung to the car door, calling harshly, "Every one of you come in here and see what we got. You'll never believe it if you don't see. You'll think I robbed you."

Chapter Nine

DAYLIGHT found them well out of the valley, swinging up a frowning canyon that wound toward the higher peaks. The country was already extremely rough, a hodgepodge of tumbled rocks, of scrubby timber, of cross canyons that created a maze through which it was difficult to keep a sense of direction.

Sawyer rode at the end of the long file of outlaws, with Wilson on his right. Throughout the two hours since they had left the train he had managed to drop small pieces of paper torn from his little notebook.

He had no way of knowing where they fell or whether the wind carried them away, but he had no chance to leave a better sign, for Wilson was there. Wilson was watchful of everything.

He stretched, easing his weight in the saddle. He had not been on a horse in more than six months, and his muscles were beginning to stiffen and ache.

Wilson turned his head. "What's the matter with you?"

Sawyer gave him a wry grin. "I'm a whiskey salesman, not a cowboy. This horse is hard."

The big man's belly shook as he laughed. The rest of the crew, strung out ahead of them, were glum, silent, sullen with the knowledge that their effort had been for nothing, that they had carried away from the holdup not one single dollar. But Jumbo Wilson was a different breed, and Sawyer realized that money meant very little to the huge man.

Why he rode with Kelly, Sawyer could only guess, but he had noted that the giant followed his leader with a dog-like devotion, and he recalled a chance remark the girl had made about her brother's ability to command loyalty from his men.

Wilson was still laughing. "Wonder if those passengers have gotten up enough nerve yet to go back to the train. They probably still think there's dynamite planted in the roadbed."

Sawyer looked at him in surprise. "Isn't there?"

Wilson's big belly shook again with his laughter. "Naw. Of course not. Why go to all that trouble? You tell a man he's sitting on a box of dynamite with a fuse lit, and he's not going to waste time looking to see if it's empty. He's going to do just what the conductor did, high-tail it away from there as fast as he can."

Sawyer thought this over. He had played it wrong, of course. The fact that the roadbed was not mined only proved it so. But what else could he have done? There had been passengers aboard who had nothing to do with the railroad and its problems. He could not have endangered their lives even if he had been certain that Kelly was bluffing. Nor would the railroad officials have thanked him for losing a locomotive and half a dozen cars.

"Lucky it wasn't," Wilson said. "When Joel found those washers he was mad enough to blow the whole shebang to pieces, just for spite. Joel's a funny guy. He's your friend, there's not a thing in the world he won't give you—except money. Joel's money-crazy. He likes to keep it around in bags and play with it, like an Injun playing with beads."

"So none of us got anything."

"We will." Wilson was supremely confident. "As long as they run trains."

"How far do we have to ride?"

"Most of the day. Wait until you see the place. The Army couldn't get in there with half a dozen cannon."

"Kelly isn't very happy with me. After this, maybe he won't need me."

"You got brains." Wilson said this with deep conviction. "It ain't often we get a guy with brains, and Joel's no fool. This was a bad shot, but there'll be others coming. Stop worrying."

Ahead of them Kelly had pulled up in a small meadow where the canyon widened until its glowering walls were a hundred feet apart.

The men were dismounting, and already one was building a fire. Sawyer and Wilson rode in and stepped down just as Virginia Kelly was lifted from her saddle by Fred Kirk.

There was a smirk on the redhead's narrow face as he set the girl on the ground, and Jumbo Wilson regarded him with attention, saying in a low voice to Sawyer, "He thinks he's a ladies' man. The boss had better watch him."

Sawyer turned as Kirk arranged a saddle blanket for the girl. He saw the smile she gave him and the color that came up under Kirk's freckled skin. Obviously Kirk was highly pleased with himself, and Sawyer wondered what Kelly's sister had said to him during the two-hour ride.

Kelly ignored her. He ignored all of them. As soon as the coffee in the blackened pot boiled, he poured himself a cup and climbed to a small rocky promontory that thrust up beside the swiftly running stream. He stood there, his back to the men eating below him, gazing off down-canyon as if he were looking for a quick pursuit.

Jumbo Wilson finished his jerked meat and beans, and cleaned his plate with a crust of pan-baked bread. Then he rose and climbed after his chief.

Kelly had squatted on his heels, and Wilson crouched down beside him. Watching them, Sawyer wondered what they talked about, if it concerned him. He was sitting on the butt of a half-rotted log, and he noted that the rest of the crew had drawn a little away from him, as if they feared that he contaminated the air merely by breathing it.

It was not only, he realized, that as far as they were concerned he was an outlander, not a member of the crew. It was also that in some obtuse way they blamed him because there had been no money in the pay car.

Aside from Kelly and Jumbo, he knew, he had not a friend in the camp, and he had the feeling that his fate was even now being decided on the rock pile above him.

He felt someone watching him, and turned to find Virginia Kelly's eyes upon him. She did not look away but continued to stare. Even at a distance of twenty yards he could feel her contempt, and he knew that he had no more rabid enemy in the place.

He found a cigar and lit it, and noted for the first time that his hands were shaking.

He knew the reason. Reaction was setting in. For days he had keyed himself for the events of this past night, and now he was completely let down by the sudden anticlimax.

Nothing had been accomplished. He was no closer to capturing Joel Kelly than he had been in Whitewater months ago.

He saw Wilson rise from his place beside the outlaw leader and clamber back down the rock pile toward him. He steeled himself for the verdict.

Jumbo stopped. He said flatly, without preamble, "You take charge of the girl."

Sawyer was startled. "I what?"

"You take charge of Joel's sister. Keep her out of his way. If she shoots off her face to him now, I think he might kill her."

Sawyer threw down his cigar. "Why pick on me?"

"Because she hates your guts." Wilson's big features were twisted into a serious frown. "Because she'd work on any of the other men. Joel knows it as well as I do. He watched her working on Fred Kirk this morning."

"Why doesn't he turn her loose?"

Wilson shook his head. "You gotta understand Kelly. The

one thing he can't stand is for someone to turn against him, anyone. He won't let her go. He'll never let her go now, and yet he can't trust her."

"Then why does he trust her with me?"

Wilson's smile was almost childlike in its simplicity. "Because she hates you almost as much as she hates Joel. Because she thinks you killed her husband."

Sawyer stared at him. This big man fooled you. Behind the heavy, almost stupid face was a brain more cunning than Sawyer had thought, weighing each situation, each human relationship.

"Did you suggest this, or did Kelly?"

Wilson preened himself. "Since you mention it, I did. I said from the first that you got brains. I ain't changed my mind."

"I've got enough brains not to want any part of her."

"What's the matter? You afraid?"

Sawyer thought that one over. Wilson was nearer the truth than he knew. Sawyer was afraid, not so much of the girl as of his own reactions to her.

That she was apparently honest in her attacks on her brother did not reassure him fully. Too many times had he seen family quarrels that healed when an outsider stepped in to make capital of them. But he said lightly, "Who's afraid of a woman?"

Wilson lost his frown, and his belly laugh rumbled out across the camp. "I am, friend. I am. I'd rather tangle with a grizzly than with that gal over there. Just you watch she doesn't slip a knife between your ribs. And watch she doesn't run out. If she does, Kelly'll have your hair."

He ambled away. Sawyer sat where he was for a long minute. Then he rose and went slowly toward where Kirk and the girl talked, close together.

Fred Kirk looked up at his approach, the green eyes in his narrow, mottled face squinting a little.

"What do you want?"

Sawyer said solidly, "I'm your relief. I'm supposed to take over the prisoner for a while."

Kirk was stretched out on the hard ground, his long legs somewhat bowed under the faded butternut pants, his scarred boots looking curiously small with their oversized spurs, his upper body raised, resting on an elbow.

In a single fluid motion he sat up, crossed his feet, and rose without using his hands.

"Who says so?"

"Kelly."

Kirk looked up where the gang boss still held his place on the jutting rocks.

"Why?"

Sawyer was watching the girl from the corner of his eye, but he gave his main attention to Kirk, sensing the man was as dangerous as a coiled rattler.

"I could tell you to ask him." His tone was even. "I'll save you the trouble. Kelly figures you're getting a little too friendly with her. He figures I won't be so much affected by her charms."

He saw color flow into the swell of her cheeks. Kirk took half a step forward, his fists knotting at his sides.

Sawyer did not move, making no effort to defend himself. "I wouldn't. I've an idea Kelly is in no mood for a fight in the crew. I've an idea Jumbo will kill you if you start anything."

Kirk's eyes clouded with bafflement.

"I'll get you." His words were soft. "Sometime when Kelly and Wilson aren't around. I'll stomp you, see."

Sawyer turned away. He heard Kirk mutter something to the girl, then saw the man move quickly to the fire. She rose. She walked to Sawyer's side and spoke very low.

"I hope you're very proud of yourself."

He was anything but that.

"I suppose you realize what you've gotten me into by holding me when I tried to get away with the rest of the passengers?"

He did realize.

"Joel's too smart." Her voice was bitter. "I might have known he'd guess what I was up to. I should have waited."

"It didn't take you long to break down Kirk."

She gave him a slow, sultry look. "Any woman can make any man do what she wants if she's willing to exert herself."

He smiled at her. "Is that a warning?"

She shook her head. "No, Mr. Sawyer. I'll never try to get you to do anything. I'd rather trust my brother than you."

Chapter Ten

THE HIDEOUT, which Joel Kelly had maintained for two years, was in a circular valley high in the Bitterroots, in some of the roughest country Sawyer had ever seen. The bowl, which he judged must be at least ten thousand feet high, was reached by a thin canyon that cut through a ridge of rock rising a thousand feet above the trail.

As they filed into the canyon, a guard loomed abruptly from the rocks above them, a rifle held ready.

"That you, Kelly?"

Kelly's voice echoed upward, the words bouncing back and forth between the canyon faces.

"It's me."

He rode on, ignoring the other armed man who had appeared on the opposite rim.

Sawyer, beside the girl in the center of the train, said in a low voice, "Looks like no one is going to surprise us while we're here."

She didn't answer. All afternoon they had ridden side by side, so close their stirrups occasionally clinked, and she hadn't spoke a word.

The bowl itself was perhaps a hundred acres in extent, a

pleasant place with a thick carpet of lush grass and a stream that wandered back and forth across it in lazy, snakelike curves.

A polé corral had been built in the center of the meadow, and around it, without pattern, a dozen cabins. The sun had dropped below the rim before they rode into the valley, but light lingered in a mauve afterglow, softening the raw buildings.

They came to the corral, and Sawyer stepped down and turned to offer his hand to the girl. She ignored it, slipping from the saddle unaided. Without a word she loosed the cinch, dragged the saddle from the horse's back, and turned the weary animal into the corral.

Kelly was still mounted. He watched her performance with a mocking smile, saying to Sawyer in a tone the girl could not help hearing, "You've got her saddle-broke already."

She turned on him, and Sawyer had never heard such anger in a woman's voice.

"Joel, don't ever let me get hold of a gun when you're around. You're a scourge. You killed Mother with what you did, and for years you made me do things I hated. But I'm free of you now."

Sawyer half-expected Kelly to step from his horse and strike her, and he realized that if Kelly did he would probably be unable to control himself. But surprisingly the bandit leader laughed. He pulled the gun from his belt and tossed it in a little arc to the girl.

She made no effort to catch it. The gun landed in the grass at her feet. She stood staring down at it as at a snake, as if her flash of anger had robbed her of the ability to move or speak.

Kelly rode over slowly, gracefully. He did something Sawyer had not believed possible. He leaned down from the saddle, picked up the gun from the ground, and righted himself all without apparent effort, and dropped the weapon into his holster.

"Your cabin's the last one up the creek. Carry her duffle up there, Sawyer."

Marc Sawyer lifted the girl's bags and without glancing at her, started for the cabin. He sensed rather than heard that she followed him, for her small feet made no sound on the green cushion of grass.

The cabin was small and surprisingly clean, a single room with a fireplace and three bunks against the opposing wall.

He set her bags in place, struck a match and lighted the single lamp. Then he went past the girl and climbed the hillside to cut a dozen fresh pine boughs. He carried them back and arranged them on the low bunk, then spread her saddle blanket over them.

He turned, saying more brusquely than he intended, "I'll bring you something to eat as soon as it's ready."

"Don't leave yet." Her voice was unsteady. "I think I'll go crazy if I'm left alone just now."

He said, still brusquely because he could not trust himself, "You're tired. You haven't had proper sleep for three days. Why don't you lie down?"

"I can't." Her face was suddenly gaunt. "I can't. I'm so damned alone. I don't want to think. I don't—" She was crying wildly. He never knew how it happened, how she came into his arms, but her fingers were biting through the cloth of his coat.

He kissed her. It was the last thing he had intended to do. She turned her head to dig her face into the protective shelter of his shoulder, but she did not try to pull away.

Finally the racking sobs lessened, and she lifted her face, looking up at him.

"You think I'm trying to use you the way I tried to use Kirk?"

"Are you?"

"No. I don't know. I didn't plan this. Now you can get out of here, and I don't want anything to eat."

He did not argue. He moved to the doorway and through it. He stopped. Fred Kirk was standing less than ten feet outside, his eyes narrow, his thin mouth an ugly line.

"Getting along pretty well, huh?"

From where the man stood, Sawyer knew, he must have seen through the open door into the lighted cabin.

"Get out of my way."

"The hell with you." Kirk's hand dropped to his holstered gun.

Sawyer did not waste time. He knew from Kirk's slurred speech that the man had been drinking. He pulled his own gun with a single sweeping gesture, swinging it up before Kirk realized what was happening.

"Get away from here." His gun was steady but no more menacing than his voice. "If I ever catch you around this cabin, I'll kill you."

Kirk started to speak, seemed to think better of it, and went stumbling across the meadow. Sawyer watched him, his face bleak, his eyes brooding, until Kirk disappeared into one of the lower cabins. Then he stuffed his gun back into place and walked to the shack where the cook was preparing the evening meal.

He ate the jerked meat and beans and pan bread without hunger or relish. He ate a little apart from the others, and half a dozen times he caught members of the crew watching him.

It was a sullen bunch, made more explosive by the stone jug that passed slowly around the fire in the open space before the cook shack.

No one offered Sawyer a drink. No one spoke to him as he carried his battered tin dish to the creek and scoured it clean. Kelly had disappeared into one of the cabins, and Wilson was not in sight.

Sawyer gathered up his blanket and saddle and carried them up the valley. He knew that everyone was watching his movements, but he paid no attention. In a small hollow some twenty feet from the girl's door, he placed the saddle on the ground, rolled himself in the blanket, and stretched out.

He was utterly weary, the tiredness running as deep as the marrow of his bones, but sleep did not come easily. He lay, his head on the saddle, his eyes wide open, staring up at the high arch of the star-milky sky.

He heard the girl come to the cabin door and knew that she stood there in the opening although the lamp inside had been extinguished. He could not guess whether or not she saw him. Finally he slept.

He came awake, the sun in his eyes, to find Jumbo Wilson standing over him, grinning.

"You take your guard job real to heart, don't you?"

Sawyer sat up.

"I saw your beef with Kirk last night. I cooled him out some. He was drunk, and when he's drinking he's a mean customer."

"Thanks."

"Don't thank me. Joel won't stand for beefs between the men."

"What's he going to do with her?" Sawyer jerked his head in the direction of the cabin.

"I don't know. I don't think he knows. She's got him stumped. He's not used to people crossing him up. How'd you like to marry her?"

Sawyer's eyes opened wide. "Marry her? Whose idea is that, yours or Kelly's?"

"Mine, but I think he'd go for it. Marry her, and he'll put up enough money for you to take her out of the country. Europe, maybe."

Sawyer started to laugh. He couldn't help it. Wilson looked startled.

"What's so funny? She ain't so bad-looking."

Sawyer shook his head. "She hates my guts, and you both know it. She thinks I killed her husband. How do you figure on making her marry me?"

Wilson shrugged. "That's easy. There's a mountain preacher over a few miles. He'd say the lines. He'd do most anything for a jug of whiskey."

"And as soon as we got out of these hills, married or not, she'd turn me over to the first sheriff we met."

"Don't worry. We'd get you safe to Mexico. Once you

were there she wouldn't have much choice but to go along. You'd have the dough. She'd be in a foreign country where she didn't even speak the language."

Sawyer felt as if he were not hearing correctly. The casual way Kelly and Wilson went ahead rearranging other people's lives to suit their own convenience appalled him. He was not a sentimentalist, his training and his long years as a man-hunter had squeezed most of his ideals out of him, but there were limits past which he had never gone to trap even the worst criminal.

It was, he thought wryly, a kind of code. It was probably this that had made him the hunter rather than the hunted, a law officer rather than a bandit.

He said slowly, "I'll have to think about it. The idea is new."

"You want money, don't you?"

That was the part he was playing, a money-hungry whiskey salesman who had been willing to throw in with Joel Kelly in the hope of personal gain.

"Give me the day."

"What is it now? Think by holding out you can up the ante?"

Somewhere he found an uneasy laugh. Somehow he made it sound convincing. "That could have something to do with it."

He watched Wilson lumber away. Later he crossed the meadow and found a place where brush had grown into a natural screen that concealed a loop of the bubbling creek. Here, long ago, beavers had thrown up a dam. The dam was gone, washed out by the flood waters of spring, but behind the remaining logs lay a pool better than waist-deep.

He stripped his clothes from his lithe body and stepped into the chill water, scrubbing at the grime left by the train ride of the last three days.

The water was numbing cold, fed by the snow that still lingered in the higher hills, and he came from the pool refreshed and vital. He viewed his shirt with distaste, but it was all he had. His baggage was still in the Spokane hotel.

He dressed slowly, picked up his gun from the ground and examined it carefully, knowing full well that his chance for survival might rest on that gun.

He had asked for the day to make up his mind. He felt that by nightfall Bob Holt would have a posse in the hills searching for the hideout.

How many men Holt would get he could not guess, but he knew that Holt would raise the country and that the railroad would not spare expense in trying to run down the gang.

He turned away from the creek and walked back to the cook shack. Four men loafed in its shade. Neither Kelly nor Wilson was in evidence.

He filled a plate, hesitated, then filled a second, and carrying them in one hand, picked up two cups of coffee with the other, and started up the creek toward the girl's cabin.

He passed the spot where he had slept and moved on toward the closed door. He tapped it with his toe, balancing the food in his hands. There was no response.

He waited, then tapped again with his toe. Still there was no answer. He looked along the winding sweep of the creek. The only place where it was sheltered from view was at the beaver dam where he had bathed. He was certain that she could not have reached it without his seeing her.

He set the food on the ground, pushed open the door, and glanced quickly around the empty cabin. Her bags stood open in the far corner and he strode to them and stared down in surprise

One was entirely empty. The other was less than half-filled.

His first thought was that she had unpacked and hung up her clothes, but a glance at the row of pegs along the wall, the only hanging space, proved them empty.

She could, of course, have been traveling light, but he doubted it. From what little he knew of women this did not seem likely. The more obvious answer was that she was trying to get away, carrying some of her things, not bothering with the heavy grips.

He stepped from the cabin and walked around it. Here the

grass grew higher, and there was a trampled path leading to the timbered slope above the meadow floor.

He stood over the marks of her passage, undecided what to do. The country she was heading into was wild and nearly uninhabited.

He could tell Kelly that she was gone so he would send men out after her, but that would only lead to further trouble. Instead, he started quickly for the timber.

Halfway between the cabin and the rising canyon wall, the stream made a wide, circling loop. The ground along its brim was marshy and soft, and in the soft ground he found not only the imprints of her small boots but also those of a man.

He stopped, thinking for an instant that someone else had already followed her. Then he saw a place where her mark was clearly superimposed over the larger footprint. He realized then that she had been walking behind the man.

Kirk. The name flashed into his mind, and he saw the redhead's narrow face as it had looked on the preceding night when they had met outside the girl's cabin.

Unconsciously he quickened his pace. He had been afraid for her before, thinking of her heading alone into the rugged hills, but now he knew she was in for greater danger.

The man was little more than an animal, utterly without morals or restraint. He tried to determine how long they had been gone. He was certain they could not have passed him while he slept. From long practice he roused at the slightest movement. Say it was half an hour since he had gone to the creek to bathe. What did Kirk hope to accomplish? The man, for all his faults, was not stupid. He would know as well as Sawyer what little chance they stood of getting through the mountains on foot.

But who said that he intended to go on foot? If this escape was a planned thing—and Sawyer now had no doubt that it was—Kirk could easily have taken two horses from the corral while the crew slept, and hidden them in the brush.

He almost turned and raced back to the camp to give the alarm. Without a horse he stood practically no chance of catching them if they were mounted. Yet he hesitated to stir up Kelly, not knowing what the man might do to the girl if he learned she had run away. Better to find out if they did have horses before he told anyone of her flight.

He came into the first of the timber and began to climb. There was no difficulty in following their progress, for they had made no effort to cover their trail. The carpet of brown needles on the rocky ground showed scuffs where their feet had disturbed it.

The trail led up a small side-draw, dry now but bearing signs that it carried run-off during the spring break-up. It rose steeply, in places so sharp he was forced to use his hands. At one point the girl had fallen and slid downhill half a dozen feet. There was a little blood on a rock, as if she had scraped an arm or leg.

The draw pinched suddenly, and he saw that she and Kirk had climbed out to the left, up a face of rock that was pitched at a seventy-degree angle. It would have been impossible to climb without the hardy trees, whose roots anchored in the crevices and offered handholds. Sawyer pulled himself upward.

He came to the top of a hogback bare of everything save some low-growing brush, and paused to recover his breath. The thin mountain air made breathing difficult even on the level, and his lungs ached with a hard constriction, as if an iron band were drawn too tightly around his chest.

Below him was another side canyon, larger than the one he had climbed, and he stiffened. He caught a glimpse of a horse tethered in the trees.

At once he dropped off the bare crest of the ridge into the shelter of the timber below, pausing to listen as soon as he was out of sight, wondering if Kirk had spotted him, wondering if the man was waiting in the lower brush, his gun ready.

And then he heard her cry, not a scream but a panting sound as if she was struggling.

"No, no, no . . ."

Chapter Eleven

HE BURST through the screening bushes into a small natural clearing. On the far side two horses stomped restlessly at the flies, unmindful of the struggle going on before them.

The girl and Kirk stood in the middle of the clearing, a dozen feet from where Sawyer broke out of the brush. Kirk's back was toward him, and he appeared to be trying to pick up the girl, bending her backward across his arm as she beat at his lowered face with her fists.

"No."

"Stop it." The man's voice was thick with heat. "Stop acting like a school kid. I saw you with Sawyer last night. Ain't I as good as him? —Or didn't you mean those promises you made me if I got you away?"

"When you get me safe away." Her voice was a sob. "Not here, not until we're safe, out of the mountains."

The man's laugh was a cruel thing. "You little fool. Did you actually think I'd wait that long? No one crosses up Fred Kirk, girlie."

She gave a sudden wrenching turn, breaking out of his grasp. He caught the shoulder of her dress, trying to pull her back. The light fabric tore, both the dress and the camisole beneath it, tore all the way to her waist.

He had her in an instant, clawing at the corset strings, trying to free her firm young body.

He was like an animal gone mad. He never heard Sawyer

as Marc charged in. He never knew that anyone was within miles until Sawyer grabbed his shoulder and spun him away from the girl, turning him like a top. Kirk's hip hit her as he spun around, and her boot heel snagged in the long grass, throwing her down.

He dropped to his knees, but he did not stay there. His eyes looked wild as he stared up at Sawyer. Then he leaped off the ground as if his knees were springs, and he lunged forward crazily, cursing as he came.

Sawyer hit him with a left and then a right, knocking him a step backward, then came closer and aimed a blow at the side of Kirk's narrow jaw.

Kirk ducked under it with surprising speed and dove forward, striking Sawyer's stomach with the point of his bony shoulder, wrapping his long arms about Sawyer's middle, digging his feet into the ground, and trying to bend Sawyer backward across his locked arms.

They went down together, rolling over and over across the grass as they struggled for an advantage. Kirk's face was close to Sawyer's, and his breath sour with stale whiskey and moist tobacco.

Somehow Sawyer broke the grip around his waist, tumbled free, and came quickly to his feet. His hand went to his holster as Kirk came up. The gun wasn't there. It had jarred loose and fallen out as they rolled.

Kirk's hand had gone to his boot top, and he straightened now, a six-inch knife in his fingers. He came in cautiously, slowly, circling, alert for an opening, the blade held point-forward in the thrusting position of a trained fighter.

Sawyer watched it grimly. He watched the whole man. But mostly he watched Kirk's feet. You could tell more quickly from a man's feet which way he would jump than you could tell from his shifting body.

He saw Kirk set himself and was ready for the diving thrust. As the man came, he sidestepped quickly, grabbing for the wrist of the knife arm, twisting, throwing the point of his hip into Kirk's side, trying to break the grip on the knife.

He failed in this, but he did succeed in throwing the man over his head.

Kirk fell heavily on his back, and Sawyer dropped on the knife arm, prying at the fingers.

The man, after the moment it took him to recover his breath, was like a snake, writhing, wriggling, at last breaking Sawyer's hold and rolling free. He came up to his knees and then to his feet.

He rose faster than Sawyer did, and he was already diving again, the blade point reaching hungrily for Sawyer's belly. Marc sidestepped at the last moment and again snared the wrist. As he did so the knifepoint gouged a long tear in his coat sleeve and into the skin beneath.

They stood thus for a long moment, close together, each straining with his full strength, Kirk to free his arm, Sawyer desperately to cling, knowing that if the arm was pulled free, Kirk would drive the steel deep into his side.

Somehow he managed to get a boot heel behind the man's knees, to knock Kirk's feet from under him as he strained at the knife, and again they went down together.

The fall jarred him, and for an instant he did not realize that the man beneath him had ceased to struggle. Then as the realization came, he lifted himself slowly.

Kirk had fallen on his own blade. The thick, heavy point had slid between the ribs as Sawyer bent his hand across his stomach. The knife had reached the heart.

He stood above the dead man, aware for the first time since the fight had started how very short of oxygen he was.

His lungs labored, fighting to drag in enough of the thin mountain air. His head whirled and he thought he would collapse. Black and red spots made a moving pattern before his eyes.

His head cleared slowly, and he was conscious of movement on his right. He turned to find Virginia Kelly standing near, her eyes enormous in the whiteness of her face.

"Is he . . . is he dead?"

Sawyer nodded. He found it impossible to speak. He

watched her, and saw her sway a little as if reaction was hitting her.

Instinctively his arms reached out to catch her, his hands grasping her bare shoulders and slipping down her back. The corset lacings were broken, and the garment curved away from her as he held her.

Without thinking, he bent and found her mouth, and suddenly she came alive, returning his kiss with a frenzy wholly unexpected as he felt a shiver pulse through her.

"Sawyer, Sawyer."

He did not hear the words but read them in the movement against his lips.

"Thank God you got here."

A sense of protective tenderness such as he had never known washed over him, leaving him weak, shaken.

"Ginny, Ginny darling."

She pushed away from him, and there was brightness in her cheeks, as if she had suddenly realized she was half-naked. She turned her back, and he saw the tracery of tiny golden freckles across her shoulders as she bent to readjust the gaping corset.

"Can you fasten me?"

. He gently tightened and tied the ends of the lace, which Kirk's clawing hands had broken. Then she pulled up the torn dress and with pins which had held the yoke in place repaired it as best she could. When she faced him again fully, the color still brightened her cheeks, but she had her voice under careful control.

"Thank you, Marc Sawyer. I don't understand you, a man who can kill another for hire and still act as you just did toward me."

"I didn't kill your husband." He was stripping off his coat, and for the first time she saw that he was cut. Her mind had been so engrossed with her own problems that she had not noticed this before.

"You're hurt." Her tone changed, and she moved quickly to examine the wound.

"Can you get your shirt off?"

He grinned at her. "It's not that bad. It hardly broke the skin." But he peeled off the shirt, and she saw that the forearm was sliced a quarter of an inch deep from wrist to elbow.

"Can you use your fingers?"

He flexed them.

She stooped then and raised her outer skirt, and he had a glimpse of her firmly rounded legs as she ripped a strip from the white petticoat.

She led him to the creek and washed the arm and bandaged it. When she had finished she looked up at him, and he again caught her by the shoulders.

"Ginny, did you hear what I said? You've got to believe it. I did not kill Floyd Pierson. The shot came from a room across the hall. It was as cleverly framed as anything I've ever seen."

She stepped back, although his hands still held her shoulders, and her face was a question as she raised it, her lips a little parted.

"You don't have to lie to me now."

"I'm not lying," he said. "I've been lying all along. I'm not a whiskey salesman, my name isn't Marc Sawyer. There is a real Marc Sawyer working for the distillery. We set it up that way in case your brother checked back on me."

"We?"

"The railroad. I'm a railroad detective."

She stood for a long moment, her face unchanging. "Did you know Floyd?"

"I'd seen him, in a Texas courtroom."

"Why didn't you tell me this before?" Her voice held doubt.

"I didn't dare. I couldn't trust you. I couldn't be sure you weren't working with your brother."

"Even after my husband was killed?"

He met her look steadily. "Even then. Remember, I had no way of knowing that you hadn't married Pierson on Kelly's orders, that it hadn't been the plan for you to find out for sure if Pierson was a railroad employee."

"You believed that of me?"

His voice roughened. "What else was I supposed to think? You are Kelly's sister. You'd come up to Wyoming to meet him."

"I'd come to beg him not to kill Floyd. Jumbo Wilson had been in Denver, watching us. I saw him. In fact I talked to him there, and he told me that my husband was a railroad detective. I knew then that he was marked for death. I know the way Joel thinks. I begged Floyd to quit, to get out of the country. He only laughed at me. He was so very, very certain of himself. Why is it that a man won't listen to caution?"

Sawyer did not answer.

She drew a long, shuddering breath, almost a sob. "So I went up to talk to Joel. I told him that if Floyd Pierson was killed I was through with him, I'd turn him in to the authorities the first chance I had.

"He promised." Her voice broke, and Sawyer saw that her hands were clenched tightly at her sides as she fought to recapture her control. "He promised. It was the first time he had ever promised me anything and deliberately broken his word.

"When he did that I realized what I should have known a long time ago, that I'd lost him completely. I'd held on all these years, thinking that I still had a small influence for good on him."

Sawyer pulled her against him and kissed her gently, feeling the convulsive shudder as it raced through her supple body.

"I'm sorry, Ginny."

She stepped away from him. "What are we going to do?"

He had been asking himself the same question. He still expected Bob Holt's posse to locate them sometime before nightfall, and he certainly did not want her at the hideout when the fight came.

Yet he could not send her into the hills alone and he knew that he should stay. It was one of the hardest decisions he had ever had to make.

He said slowly, "Wilson came to me this morning with a proposition. He wanted me to marry you."

She stared at him in surprise. "Jumbo Wilson wanted you to marry me? Why?"

He grinned a little. "Because you're beginning to worry Kelly. Wilson offered me money to marry you, a lot of money if I'd take you to Europe."

"But how?"

He told her what Wilson had told him.

"Is this Joel's idea?"

"I don't think so, but Jumbo has a way of selling your brother on his ideas. I suspect Joel would go along."

"Are you asking me to marry you?"

He had to laugh in spite of the depth of his emotion. "That's probably as strange a proposal as you'll ever get. If the question is Do I want to marry you? the answer is Yes. I think I have from that first night in Whitewater, but I never expected to have the chance."

With a little cry she was in his arms again. "Sawyer, oh, Sawyer. I never expected to find another man after Floyd."

"Did you love him very much?" He knew a quick, sharp flush of jealousy.

"Yes." It was a single word, and he was left to make of it what he could.

"But you will marry me?"

"I would even if I didn't love you, and I think I do. This has come too fast for me to understand exactly what's happening to me."

"All right." He became businesslike; their time was short, and he had made up his mind. No matter what he owed the railroad, he felt he owed this girl more. He had to get her away before the posse closed in. Later, if he had found a place where she would be out of harm's way, he would circle back to help.

"Do you have other clothes? I noticed that your bags at the cabin were empty."

"In the saddlebags. I was just putting them there when Kirk grabbed me. I think he never meant to take me away. I think he planned from the first to do just as he did."

She turned and moved toward the horses, her torn dress

pulling loose from the pins as she walked. She found another
dress and disappeared in the sheltering brush to change.

When she returned she had straightened her hair, and he
was again amazed at how fresh and attractive this girl could
be no matter what the circumstances.

He left the horses where they were tied. Returning them
would only raise questions he did not want to answer, and
they might need the animals later.

He helped her climb the hogback and retrace the trail up
which they had come.

"One thing," he warned her, "don't let your brother guess
that you want to marry me, that there is anything at all between us. If he thought for one moment that we had made arrangements of any kind, I'd never get out of this place alive."

Chapter Twelve

THEY REACHED the timbered lip of the bowl and peered
out at the rear of her cabin. As far as Sawyer could see there
was no one near, and he led the girl forward quickly, hoping
they would escape detection.

They gained the corner of the log building, rounded it, and
slipped through the doorway. Not until they were within the
dim interior did they realize the cabin was not empty.

Joel Kelly sat on the lower bunk, his legs crossed, a pipe
burning between his lips. His smooth, handsome face was
empty of expression, as if he had consciously drained away his
thoughts.

"Where have you two been?"

Sawyer recovered almost instantly, alert to danger. The girl stood speechless, her dread of her brother filling the small room.

"Your sister decided to take off." Sawyer's tone was casual, almost bored. "I brought her back."

"I thought you would." It was impossible to judge from Kelly's tone exactly what the man meant. There was usually that mockery in the smooth voice.

"So you thought you could run away?"

She glanced at Sawyer as if for help, but found none. His eyes were fixed on the rough floor between his booted feet.

"What did you expect me to do?" She sounded defiant.

"I expected you to have a little sense. How long do you think you'd last in those hills?"

"What difference does it make to you? I'd be out of your way, out of your hair. Isn't that what you want?"

He came off the bunk in one sweeping movement. Sawyer expected him to strike the girl and set himself. This time he meant to beat Kelly within an inch of his life, perhaps to kill him.

The idea came with sudden clarity, and he wondered why it had taken so long. It would solve so many things if Joel Kelly were dead.

But Kelly did not strike his sister. He grasped her by the shoulders, holding her firmly yet with a curious gentleness that Sawyer had never observed in him before.

"You belong to me." There was no mockery in the voice now, only a flat quality that spoke of truth. "You can hate me, despise me, but you still belong to me, and I never let go of anything that is mine, not anything."

His voice had risen as he talked, and his eyes, as they came up past the girl's head to stab at Sawyer, were not quite sane.

Sawyer caught his breath. This possessiveness, this love of concrete things, was an obsession with the bandit, a driving force carried beyond reason, beyond conscious thought.

Kelly was speaking again, his tone lowered, matter-of-fact, as if he was utterly unaware that for an instant his self-control had been stripped away.

"Sawyer."

"Yes?"

"You remember what Wilson talked to you about this morning?"

"I know." He saw the girl stiffen slightly in her brother's arms.

"What about it?"

Sawyer made his voice callous. "How much?"

Kelly laughed. "You hear that?" He was speaking to his sister. "You don't know what we're talking about, do you? Well, I'll tell you. He's going to marry you. You'd think a man offered a chance like that would show some interest, wouldn't you? But all he cares about is money. I wish you happiness."

"Joel. You can't mean a thing like that?" The girl sounded horrified, and Sawyer wondered momentarily if she was only acting.

Kelly's voice was tense. "I mean just that. I've got to keep you in hand, and I don't know how else to do it. You'll marry him, and we'll ship you to Europe, out through Mexico. And you'll stay with him because he'll have the money. Without him you'll starve. Women don't go running around Europe without funds. It isn't the United States."

"And if I won't?"

"You will." It was a flat statement. "If you don't, I'll turn you over to the men, one at a time."

Sawyer thought that if he and the girl had not already had their talk, he would have killed Kelly now. But she still played her part. She pulled away from her brother and turned on Sawyer.

"I think you know how much I despise you. Knowing how I feel, will you be a party to this outrage?"

He made his tone as cynical as possible. "If there's enough money involved."

Kelly's laughter filled the cabin. "I like this man. He keeps his eye on the main chance. Sawyer, when you get to Paris my bankers will pay you fifty thousand dollars. I'll give you enough to get there, and then you'll have to prove to them that my sister is still with you if you want to collect."

"And what's to prevent him from collecting the money and deserting me?" It was the girl.

Kelly quit laughing, and his tone turned flat. "He won't try anything like that, I promise you. He knows exactly what would happen to him if he did. But if you're smart, you'll make it so he won't want to leave you. A woman who can't hold a man is hardly worth bothering about. It's a deal, Sawyer?"

Marc Sawyer nodded slowly. "I guess so. I'd be a fool to turn it down."

"There's one more thing." Kelly sounded careless, as if what he was about to say held slight importance. "A little job you'll do for us first."

"What job?"

"We're going after Tupper."

Sawyer had to cast back quickly to remember who Tupper was. Then he shook his head. "Why? Tupper most likely skipped out before this."

Kelly grunted. "Why should he? Who's to know he stole that money and filled the sacks with washers? He'll sit in that bank right where he is. I know the man."

Sawyer was silent.

"So we're going to get him, and we're going to get that money if we have to ride into Spokane after it."

"That's crazy."

Kelly's eyes blazed. "Don't you ever use that word to me." He came a half step forward, as if he meant to strike Sawyer in the face, then with obvious effort recovered his control.

"Never mind. We'll set it up and get you to the railroad. If anyone questions you as to what happened, why you rode away with us, tell them you were kidnaped and just managed to make your escape."

"When do I leave?" Sawyer was conscious that the girl was watching him, that terror was growing in her eyes.

"As soon as you can. Get to Spokane and tell Tupper he's got twenty-four hours to turn over the money."

"What if he says he hasn't got it, that he didn't take it?"

"Then he'd better dig up fifty thousand dollars. Tell him if he doesn't, we'll come in and take his hide. He knows me. He knows about one man who crossed me and thought he was safe in prison. That man lived two weeks."

He started for the door, and at that moment the flat *spat* of a rifle shot broke the quiet of the bowl. It was followed by a second and then a third. Sawyer had never seen anyone move as fast as Joel Kelly did. The bandit leader was through the cabin entrance and running swiftly toward the cook shack before the last echoes of the first shot had fully blended with the others.

Virginia Kelly said sharply, "What is it?"

"The posse." Half a dozen more shots punctuated Sawyer's words, and he jumped toward the door in time to see Kelly's men furiously dragging their horses from the corral and throwing saddles onto them.

"We've got to get you out of here." He was already running toward the spot where he had slept, toward his saddle and rifle.

And then he saw Wilson riding up the slope toward him, leading two horses, one already saddled. The big man's face was red, but he seemed in no greater hurry than usual.

He reined in beside Sawyer, saying in a calm voice, "I saddled the girl's horse. Let's get going."

Sawyer adjusted his blanket quickly, flung up the saddle, and mounted in less than two minutes. Virginia Kelly was on her horse, quieting the nervous animal with a sure, steady touch.

"Which way?"

Wilson waved a big hand toward the right rim of the bowl. "Up there, and don't hurry. The boys at the gap will hold them for a while. The bastards will wish they'd never caught up with Joel Kelly."

"How many are there?"

Jumbo Wilson's grin was wolfish. "Didn't count 'em, but we will. Joel knows these hills like the palm of his hand. Quit worrying."

He rode out, and Sawyer and the girl exchanged quick

looks. Then she fell in behind Wilson, and Sawyer brought up the rear.

Below them the firing had increased. It now sounded like a skirmish battle. Sawyer tried and failed to guess from the number of shots how many men Holt had brought against the hideout.

They were entering the timber when he looked back and saw a string of mounted men riding toward them.

They climbed up a small canyon, then scaled the wall on what had probably been a deer trail, though it now was marked by heavy use from Kelly's men.

At a slanting hogback they turned and followed it up and over the timbered rim, then dropped down into a tiny valley north of the hideout bowl.

Behind them the sounds of firing grew indistinct, muffled by the trees and the intervening ridge. Wilson pulled up beside a trickling creek and let his horse drink.

Watching the back trail, Sawyer saw the riders drop off the ridge one by one and form an uneasy circle in the little valley's center. The last to appear was Kelly. He dropped down the slope and pushed through the rough ring of his men to Wilson's side, his face a somber mask.

"The boys are holding them at the gorge, but the posse is circling them. They'll be outflanked within an hour."

"How many?"

"Too many." Kelly swore softly under his breath. "Looks like the whole country turned out. There must be a hundred, maybe more."

Around him his men stirred restlessly. There was not one among them with the exception of Sawyer who did not have a price on his head, a picture on a wanted poster somewhere.

Sawyer slumped in his saddle, watching them, weighing them, hard cases all. He wondered, as he often did, what had turned each onto the outlaw trail.

He saw them eying Kelly, waiting for him to figure a way out of this trouble.

At their backs, cutting them off from the lower country to the east, was a force too strong for them to fight. Before them loomed the high mountains, still snow-covered, still nearly impassable.

North lay Canada if they could break through as far as the border, but Sawyer had no doubt that Bob Holt had already shut off this avenue.

He could read their minds. Their impulse was to scatter, each man to seek his own safety. Here was the test of Kelly's leadership. Could he hold his men together in the face of hopeless odds?

As if in answer to his thoughts, Kelly began giving orders.

"Crown, you and Gorman circle around Cattrap Peak. See if you can catch them from the rear. Bryce, take Eason with you and cut through the shoulder. Don't shoot unless you have a target.

"Wilson, ride up to the lookout and pull the boys out of there. The rest of you get back on the ridge. Fan out, and when the bastards ride into the bowl, let them have it. Any time some tin-star marshal thinks he's about to dig Joel Kelly out of the hills it's time to teach him a lesson."

They wheeled without a word and rode to obey. Such was the power Kelly held over these usually leaderless men.

Kelly twisted in his saddle to stare at Sawyer and his sister, to say in a bitter voice, "I wish both of you were a thousand miles from here. We could use your gun on the ridge, Sawyer, but what would we do with her?"

"We could tie her up down here, out of the way of any stray bullets."

"No. Bring her along." Kelly caught his horse around and headed back up the slope.

Sawyer wasted a minute debating whether to take the girl and chance a run for freedom, but he knew that Kelly would not hesitate a single instant if he thought they were trying to escape.

The bandit led the way without a sign of uncertainty, as if he had chosen his spot long before, and when they reached the rim Sawyer realized that there was, indeed, a prearranged plan. Just short of the rim, they rode into a small, rock-bordered clearing where a dozen horses stood hobbled, in the care of a single man.

They swung down and Sawyer, matching Kelly's action, pulled his rifle from his saddle boot. With the girl at his side, they worked around the rocks until they were abruptly at the rim.

Here the cliffs fell away at a ninety-degree angle, their stubby timber wind-twisted and gnarled so that they were little taller than bushes.

To the right, three hundred feet below, the cabins clustered around the cook shack. On the left wound the entrance of the bowl, the fully exposed point at which the gorge widened into the amphitheater. Through this the posse would most probably ride.

The sound of firing had ceased. Apparently Wilson had pulled the lookouts back from the lips of the gorge.

Sawyer crawled forward and peered down. On either side of him, spaced half a dozen feet apart, bellied down among the rocks of the rim, the outlaws waited, every rifle ready. The world was quiet.

It was a perfect trap. Sawyer fought a sickness, thinking of Holt and his posse riding blindly into it.

He readied his own rifle, and got the girl onto her stomach and lay down at her side.

Kelly passed behind them, patrolling his skirmish line, giving sharp, clear, calm orders.

"Don't shoot until I give the word. I want as many of them inside the bowl as I can get before a shot is fired."

They waited. The sun above them was hot. It beat into them with increasing intensity, and the flies were bad. Sawyer heard the girl slap at one, and turned to give her a smile of encouragement.

She smiled back. Between them was an unspoken intimacy such as Sawyer had never known. She reached out to touch his shoulder, a small gesture meaningless to anyone else but a sign of confidence, of trust, of encouragement, to him.

It sharpened his sense of loneliness, pointing up the long,

empty years, the endless trails, the chases that had had no concrete meaning for him.

Suddenly he was alert. A rider had appeared below, coming cautiously out of the canyon mouth. The man halted his horse, studied the clump of buildings, and then rode forward, still cautious, to examine the timbered slopes. Even at this distance Sawyer recognized Bob Holt.

Deliberately Holt continued past the cook shack and on up the bowl to the cabin the girl had occupied. Here he circled, looking down at the grass where the outlaws had trampled it flat in their passage.

Then, as if satisfied that the bowl held no danger, Holt turned back and hastened to the canyon entrance. Wheeling there, he motioned with a wide wave of his arm.

Sawyer raised his rifle, sighting well above Holt's head, planning a shot that would warn the posse of its danger. He knew that in so doing he risked Kelly's anger, risked perhaps death for himself, but he could not sit by and see men slaughtered by the outlaws' fire.

He never pulled the trigger. Suddenly Kelly was beside him, snatching the rifle from his grasp, swinging it by the barrel, bringing the polished stock crashing against Sawyer's head.

The blow knocked him sidewise, and he rolled to his back, too stunned to move, too stunned even to make a sound.

He lay still, knowing that Kelly stood over him, his rifle poised for a second blow, his face murderous. But the blow did not come. Kelly, as if realizing that Sawyer was in no condition to cause him further trouble at the moment, swung away.

The girl was at Sawyer's side in an instant, raising him to cradle his battered head in her lap, murmuring words he could not catch.

No one's attention was on them now, for a string of riders had filed into the bowl and were huddled in conference before the cook shack.

The volley, when it came, was deafening. It tore apart the quiet of the mountains, bouncing a thunder of echoes back and forth between the upthrust rocks.

Sawyer struggled to sit up. His head was still spinning, but the horror of the massacre below drove all else from his consciousness.

Men were down and thrashing. The horses that had not been hit plunged wildly as their riders tried to control them. Three or four of the posse were running for the shelter of the cabins. Others had wheeled and now rode desperately for the gorge.

From the heights above them Wilson and the lookouts he had pulled back loosed their fire, catching the fleeing men in a cross barrage. They wheeled again and drove in panic for the cabins. A few of them made it safely.

Those who had gained the protection of the buildings set up an answer to Kelly's ambush. Their fire searched the rocks and timber along the crest of the ridge. An outlaw on Sawyer's right cried out sharply as a bullet knocked him backward from the doubtful shield of his rock.

Another went down at the far end of the line. Sawyer twisted and found the girl sitting at his side. He pushed her behind a rock pillar and rolled to join her in a slight depression masked from the guns below.

Suddenly Kelly's voice rode over the crackle of the guns.

"All right. They've had enough. Back to the horses."

Below them in the bowl better than twenty men lay unmoving on the grass, which only a short time before had been so green.

Chapter Thirteen

EVEN the hardened men who gathered around the horses on the ridge were sobered by the carnage they had made in the bowl.

Jumbo Wilson rode in with the lookouts. The men Kelly had sent out as flankers straggled up one at a time until the full crew was gathered.

The gang had lost only three men, but what they had done that afternoon would ring through the West and mark Kelly as the most wanted outlaw of his time.

The only person seemingly unaffected was Kelly himself. Even Wilson, who usually showed no sign of emotion, was thoroughly quieted.

He walked to where Kelly stood, sliding his rifle into place, and said in a tone that, although low for him, carried to the ears of the listening men, "We gotta get out of here, Joel. As soon as the news of this fight spreads around, the country will be alive with deputy marshals."

Kelly looked at him coldly. He glanced toward where Sawyer was helping Virginia into the saddle. He had not spoken to Sawyer since he'd slammed him with the rifle butt.

"You afraid of something? The place was alive with posse men, and we handled them. We can handle anything they want to throw against us."

"You got it wrong." Wilson was very earnest. "The reason we've lasted as long as we have is that most of the small ranchers and mountaineers have been on our side—or at least they liked us better than they liked the railroads.

"But those men we killed down there were likely mostly local. There wasn't time for the railroad to bring in outsiders. They're going to have fathers and brothers and kin."

"So what can they do?"

For the first time since Sawyer had known him, Wilson was losing patience with his leader. "Look, Joel, use your head. In this country you need food to stay alive. You can't depend on what you hunt, not for this many men."

"We've always gotten food."

"That's what I'm trying to tell you. We've always been able to ride up to a cabin or a little ranch and they'd feed us, either because they were friendly or because they were afraid of us.'"

"They're still afraid of us. What's the matter, Jumbo, losing your nerve?"

One of the grouped men spoke cautiously. "Seems like he's making real good sense, Joel. This country is hot. It's time to pull stakes, if you ask me, at least until it cools down some."

Kelly spun around. His lithe body folded into a crouch, and his hand moved very near his holstered gun.

"Stop it." It was Wilson. He stood on Kelly's right, quartered to him so that Kelly would have to turn away from the man he faced to look at Jumbo.

Kelly didn't turn. He was motionless, a coiled spring, compressed and ready to expand with blinding speed.

"I mean it." Wilson drew his own gun deliberately. "Touch it, Joel, and I'll shoot you."

Kelly did turn then, recognizing that the man he faced was far less dangerous than Wilson.

"What's got into you?" He sounded surprised. He was surprised. He would not have been more startled had his horse talked back to him. They had ridden together for nearly four years, and in that time the big man had never refused to carry out an order, had never once refused a request that Kelly had made.

"Maybe I'm getting some sense. Maybe I'm just getting

scared. But we'll get no place shooting at each other. We've got to hang together, and we've got to get out of here, fast."

An applauding murmur rose from the men. Kelly looked about him, his eyes smoky with deep hatred. He spotted Sawyer, and his face hardened with purpose.

Sawyer had turned to glance at the girl. When he looked back, Kelly was standing three feet from him. Sawyer could read the man's mind.

Kelly's authority had been challenged, and he dared not strike back lest he unite the full crew against him. But Sawyer was an outsider. Most of the riders viewed him with both suspicion and dislike. Kelly could safely repair his damaged ego by an attack on Sawyer.

"Why'd you start to shoot that rifle before I gave the word?"

Sawyer watched him. His head still ached, and there was a welt an inch thick over his ear where the rifle stock had struck him.

"I wasn't going to fire, Joel." His tone was low but without apology. "I was just testing the sights. Remember, I'm a whiskey salesman. I'm not used to guns."

"You're a liar."

From the corner of his eye Sawyer saw that the rest of the crew was tensed, waiting. They did not interfere, but they showed no concern over what might happen to him.

Wilson still held his gun, but now the heavy barrel pointed downward at the ground between his worn boots.

His face was neutral, expressionless.

"Joel, stop it." The girl was already mounted. Now she slipped from her saddle and took three quick steps to place her small body between the two men.

Sawyer's impulse had been to go for his gun. He did not know if he was faster than Kelly, but he had no intention of standing and taking anything more from the bandit.

But the girl had been too close to the line of fire, and he could not chance her safety. Now it was worse. She was between them, grabbing her brother by the edge of his coat, trying to shake him.

"Listen to me, you murderer. Haven't you killed enough men for one day? Give me your gun."

Kelly struck her then, using the back of his hand in a sweeping blow that knocked her stumbling half a dozen feet before she fell.

And in the second when Kelly's eyes involuntarily turned to follow the falling girl, Sawyer took two quick, catlike steps and struck, driving his fist to the hinge of Kelly's jaw.

At the last instant, more from instinct than from thought, Kelly moved his head, so that instead of landing solidly, Sawyer's blow glanced along the cheek to almost tear an ear from the outlaw's head.

Kelly dropped to his knees, but he sprang up as if the ground were a trampolin and charged Sawyer with a scream of utter rage that might well have come from a woman.

Sawyer had the instant to set himself, and he hit the hurtling man twice, a deep right into the stomach, a clubbing left to the side of the head.

Kelly was again on his knees. This time he did not try to rise but reached out suddenly to seize Sawyer's right leg and jerk it from under him.

Sawyer went down, and Kelly's hand came out, his fingers wide-spread, straining for his opponent's eyes.

Sawyer used both hands to claw the gouging fingers away and had a swift glance at Kelly's face, twisted with pain from the belly blow, before a huge paw snared Kelly and dragged him away and Jumbo Wilson's grumbling voice rolled out savagely.

"That's enough. Quit it, both of you." He used his other hand to haul Sawyer to his feet and stood gripping them both, ready to knock their heads together.

Kelly's face looked drawn. There was a thin white circle around his lips and his eyes were not quite sane, but while Sawyer watched a change transpired, a masking curtain dropped, and when Kelly spoke again he was in full control of himself.

"All right. Let me go."

Wilson, sensing the crisis had passed, released his hold on his leader's shoulder and glanced at Sawyer.

"Had enough?"

Sawyer did not trust himself to speak. His dislike of Kelly had been building into a deep hatred more intense than any he had ever known. He merely nodded and turned away as he felt the fingers on his arm relax. He walked over to help the girl to her feet.

Kelly, paying no more attention to them than if they did not exist, went to face the grouped men. He said in a tight voice, "We've ridden together for a long time, and I've never led you wrong yet. And if you'll listen to me, I won't lead you wrong now."

They were sullen, unresponsive, and one man in the rear of the circle found the courage to say, "Sure, but we've never been in this kind of a jackpot before Let's get out of the country while we can. Let's head for Canada."

There was a murmur of agreement, and Jumbo Wilson added his voice.

"Why not, Joel? We don't gain anything just hiding in these hills. There's nothing here. Let's lay low for a while, or even pull out."

"Who said we were going to stay in the hills? We're going to Spokane."

"Spokane?" It was Wilson who spoke. Everyone else was staring.

"You don't think I'm going to let Tupper get away with that money, do you? Besides, everyone will expect us to head for the border. It will never occur to anyone that we'd go west."

They were listening now. Even Sawyer had turned. The thing he did not want was for Kelly to get away, to vanish into the wilds of western Canada. Now, no matter what happened, he meant to bring the man to justice. After the slaughter in the bowl that afternoon, all softness was wiped away. Even the girl, and the fact that the murderer was her brother, were of no importance.

Sawyer waited for the men's reaction, not daring to speak

himself. The way Kelly felt about him now, a word from him could change the outlaw's mind.

Wilson said slowly, "That makes a little sense, but how do we know Tupper hasn't taken out for the Orient?"

"Why should he? He thinks he's safe. He'll figure that when we found the washers we'd blame the railroad."

Wilson considered this slowly. "It sounds all right, but where do we cross the river?"

"Bartlett's. He's one of the few men in the country we can trust."

"I wouldn't trust even him after today. What do we do when we get to the Falls?"

Kelly turned. Sawyer was standing beside the girl, unconsciously holding her arm protectingly. Kelly studied him and then the girl, and the small mocking smile that Sawyer had come to associate with the man was back on his lips.

"We'll manage," he told Wilson. "We'll think of something. Come on, let's ride."

Better than half the crew still refused to mount. They stood sullen, defiant. From his place in the saddle, Kelly looked them over, his face sharp with contempt.

"Go on, ride north or south, or to hell. I hope you all dance at the end of a rope before you finish."

He pulled his horse around and led out, straight in the saddle, a figure from another era, a corsair, a freebooter, a buccaneer who should have been on a pirate ship, not riding across the badlands of the United States.

Chapter Fourteen

SIX RIDERS stayed with Kelly and Jumbo Wilson. Jumbo rode out at Kelly's side, but as they wound down the mountain he dropped back along the line to pull in with Sawyer and Virginia Kelly, eying them sidewise although appearing not to.

Sawyer was conscious of the scrutiny and wondered what had happened now.

"Kind of like her, don't you?"

Sawyer flicked a glance toward the girl and saw the red coming up under the even sunburn of her smooth cheeks. He took his time to answer, trying to guess at what was in the big man's mind.

"She's okay."

Wilson's reply was a dry chuckle that rumbled from his huge throat. "I guess Joel was right, at that."

"Right about what?"

"He said she must have been working on you, that the way you took care of her up on the ridge and the way you slammed into him when he slapped her showed how far gone you are."

Sawyer did not dare look at the girl. He had no idea how revealing his own face was, but he was certain that hers was scarlet.

He said shortly, "He's crazy."

"Like a fox." The big man seemed to have forgotten his shock at the massacre in the bowl, to have regained all his confidence in Joel Kelly. "That's him, thinking all the time, planning, using every angle. You know something, he didn't trust you after the way you started to fire that rifle up on the range."

As he spoke, Wilson leaned across and casually lifted Sawyer's rifle from its boot, then just as casually pulled the short gun from Sawyer's holster.

"No offense," he said. "Just helps to keep Joel's peace of mind. It's getting a little thin. The way you lit into him didn't make him love you any more. Joel likes to think he can whip any man alive except me. He knows he can't handle me, so he don't even try."

Sawyer did not protest. He rode in silence, wondering what was coming next. He had not long to wait.

Wilson laughed. "Joel's going to use you anyhow. He's sending you into Spokane to get Tupper. He don't have any fear about it because he's going to hold her, and if you try to cross us you can make a guess what will happen to her."

Sawyer turned to look at the girl. He could not help himself. She was staring straight ahead at her horse's ears, her color high but her face without expression.

"Just think about it," Wilson went on, "for the next hundred and fifty miles. Do what Joel wants done in Spokane, and you two can ride out, without money. Joel's changed his mind. He figures that now you want her so much he don't need to pay you to take her off his hands."

He touched his horse with a spur and surged ahead along the line of riders to rejoin Kelly.

"I've certainly gotten you into trouble."

He looked at her.

"If I hadn't followed you, none of this would have happened."

"I'm glad you did." His voice was far from steady. "I've never known anyone quite like you. If we had to go through this in order to meet, then that's the way it is. I've always thought that men who let their guard down entirely with women were fools. I didn't realize that the only trouble with me was that I hadn't met the right woman."

She swung her horse nearer to his and reached out to clasp her small hand over his. It told him far more than any words she might have used.

Later, when they had ridden in silence for nearly two miles, she said in a small voice, "What are you going to do?"

He did not know. Through the years he had been in a dozen tight places, situations where there had seemed no way out, yet he had found a way. But this was different. There was not only himself to concern him. The girl's safety meant far more to him than his own, or than the hope of capturing anyone.

Kelly pushed the pace, trying to put as much distance as possible between himself and the hideout with its population of dead.

They climbed, and the country roughened and the air thinned out. The sun dropped behind the peaks, and chill crept down with the blue shadows, striking through them all with the sharpness of a keen-bladed knife.

Darkness finally buried the rocky, uncertain trail, and the line hauled up. The men dismounted, and while one built a tiny fire and set coffee to boil, they gnawed at the cold biscuits and jerked meat from their saddlebags.

Sawyer located a low rock reef that thrust out of the canyon side, offering a slight shelter from the sweep of the icy downdraft, and carried his and the girl's blankets behind it.

She was shivering, and he draped both blankets about her shoulders before moving to the fire for coffee. He brought the hot liquid back to her, conscious of the crew's cautious glances, of the smirk on Kelly's handsome face.

He ignored them all, aware only of the girl, the pallor of her skin, the circles that fatigue had laid beneath her eyes. In the deepening purple of twilight she looked like a hungry lost child.

She drank the coffee and shuddered, its warmth only accentuating the chill seeping into her. He tucked the blankets closer about her and spoke against her cheek, his words so low that they were all but lost in the constant swoop of wind.

"Get a little rest."

"I'm so terribly cold."

He held her then, tight in his arms, trying to transmit the heat of his body to hers.

"Listen to me, darling. Get a little sleep. As soon as the camp settles down we'll try to slip away."

She pulled back in surprise. "Away? Where?"

"Back the trail we came. If we can make it to the hideout, we may locate what's left of the posse. If not, those two horses Kirk staked out should still be near where we left them. They were hobbled, they couldn't drift too far, and I don't dare take horses from here. If only Wilson hadn't lifted my guns."

She said, "You mean we'll walk?"

He nodded. It was now so dark that she would not have understood except for the movement of his head against her cheek.

"There's no other way. Your brother and Wilson aren't fools; they'd hear a horse leaving before we'd gone a hundred feet."

She clung to him, then opened the blankets to shelter him, and he felt warmth return to her supple body, felt the tension flow out of it, and knew finally that she slept.

He lay beside her, not wanting to move lest he rouse her.

A rock dug into his shoulder. His arm beneath her head began to cramp, but he did not move. It was black dark in the canyon bottom, with three hours ahead before the moon would rise high enough to clear the rim above them. The chilling cold crept through the blankets, numbing him, deadening his senses.

He had to fight off sleep. He watched the little fire burn down, watched the hunched shape of the single guard beyond the blaze, watched with intense concentration.

The man rose, stomped his feet and swung his arms in an effort to maintain circulation. Then he settled back and lighted a pipe. After a while he set it aside and gradually ceased to move. Sawyer judged he was asleep.

He waited ten dragging minutes to be sure. Then he wakened the girl, holding his mouth close to hers to mute any sound that might escape her.

She wakened slowly, her senses still drugged by deep fatigue. When she realized where she was, who held her tightly, she kissed him with a little murmur that held no words and needed none.

"It's time to go." He whispered it, stirring to ease back the blankets, to rise and help her to her feet, and as he moved he watched the guard.

The man did not move. The fire was a dull ember, its glow hardly touching the quiet form. The black dark of the canyon was barely pierced by starlight.

Sawyer took the girl's hand and led her, feeling his way step by step, to the edge of the timber, into its shelter, up the sharp pitch of the canyon side. He had not taken the blankets. The less they carried, the faster they could travel.

He judged they were about twenty-five miles from the massacre bowl, but the trail they had traveled was rough and paved with sharp, shattered rock.

The canyon wall steepened as they climbed inch by inch, grasping at roots, at tree trunks, at anything that lent a little leverage. It was doubly slow, for they must make as little noise as possible.

Two hundred feet above the canyon floor they paused for breath. Cold as it was, Sawyer felt the sweat form within his clothes. The girl was panting from the exertion.

Now they turned along the wall, making a cautious detour around the camp. Well beyond it they headed downward again, toward the trail. The descent was even harder than the climb had been, and twice loose rocks rolled beneath the girl's foot and pitched her into what would have been a plunging fall had not Sawyer grabbed her.

They bottomed out at last into the comparative smoothness of the path, feeling it under their feet more than seeing it. They worked their way down the canyon, crossed a small hogback, and began again to climb.

They walked in silence, hoarding their breath. Sawyer's arm was about the girl, lending her his balance, taking part of her weight, as she stumbled over the flinty rocks.

The moon was not yet over the rim, but its glow softened

the darkness of the eastern sky, seeming to increase rather than lessen the darkness of the narrow canyon.

Twice the girl sagged to the ground and lay there drinking in deep breaths. Twice Sawyer lifted her gently to her feet and moved her onward, almost like a sleepwalker.

She stumbled down for the third time and lay still, moaning softly in the misery of exhaustion.

"I can't go on. I can't, I can't. The altitude is too much."

He ran his hand across her face, feeling the flush of her quick-risen fever, knowing she was suffering from lack of oxygen.

They were two miles from the camp, perhaps three. They had to be a lot farther away by daylight if they were to have any chance for escape.

He lifted her in his arms and carried her. The grade stiffened and the trail began to switchback up the long slope of a ridge.

He remembered riding down it that afternoon, and now he wondered if he would ever reach the top. Step by step his feet grew heavier, as if someone were gradually pouring lead into his boots.

The boots had not been made for walking. Already there were blisters on both heels, and his feet had begun to swell. Each step brought increased agony.

The girl's arm was tight about his neck. He stopped and eased her down, then rested a moment, his lungs fighting for the thin air.

He knew how deathly ill she felt, but her shaky voice was determined. "Let me walk. I can walk now. You can't carry me forever."

They went on again, and suddenly the moon bloomed on the ridge crest, throwing the canyon into metallic relief. It was easier to walk in the light. They no longer strayed from the faint trace, no longer stumbled over unseen rocks and stepped down suddenly into unexpected depressions.

Their rest periods grew longer, the intervals of walking shorter, but finally they topped the ridge and saw spread out before them the massive jumble of mountains under the whey light of the moon.

It was an awe-inspiring sight, but the wild beauty was lost on Sawyer. He saw only the frightening maze they must traverse before they reached safety.

They sat down, dropping their backs against the roughness of a boulder, still not speaking, racked by their labored breathing. When it had quieted he looked at the girl and saw that her eyes were closed. He touched her arm.

"It's time to go," he said gently.

Never afterward could he remember how many times he had used that phrase through the seemingly endless night. They halted and went on, halted and went on, plodding forward, their minds numbed, their feet making the slow steps from habit only.

They reached a river they had easily forded that afternoon, the water running waist-deep over a rippled gravel bar.

Now Sawyer eyed it for long moments of dismay. Above them it dropped off the canyon wall in a boiling cascade, making a crossing there impossible. Below them it curved into a series of deep pools.

There was no help for it. He sat down and pulled the boots from his blistered feet. His socks had stuck to the raw places, and he grimaced as he worked them free. Then he stood up to strip off his pants.

He tucked up the skirt of his coat and shirt, and rolled his clothes into a neat bundle, which he handed wordlessly to the girl. Then he picked her up and stepped gingerly into the icy water.

It numbed him before he had taken half a dozen cautious steps, but at least it killed the burning in his tortured feet. The current was swift and several times he was almost swept off his feet, but finally he was through the thirty-foot swirl and lurched up the slope of the far bank. He lowered himself and the girl to the dry ground.

His legs had no feeling. He peeled off his shirt to use as a towel and rubbed circulation back into his limbs. Then he shrugged into his clothes, his teeth rattling with a chill.

It took minutes to work his feet back into the boots, and for a sinking moment he feared it was impossible.

A streak of light in the eastern sky widened and reached up to mingle with the moon's glow.

Somewhere far off in the predawn a cat cried, and the girl clutched his arm in fear.

"What was that?"

His voice was as reassuring as he could make it. "Don't worry, he wants no more to do with us than we want with him. We have more dangerous things to think about than a mountain cat hunting his breakfast. We've got to get off this trail by daylight and find a place to rest and hide."

They found a place, a rock slide where the native stone had split into jagged fragments, some as large as a house, that were jumbled together as if a massive hand had fractured them in a monstrous, crushing grasp.

The trail skirted the base of the slide. They worked up it slowly, perhaps a hundred feet, and located a sheltered, room-sized spot hemmed in on all sides by rocks that rose to form a natural parapet.

There they settled, thankful for the growing warmth of the rising sun, huddled in each other's arms. They were asleep almost at once, drugged into unconsciousness by the night's fatigue.

Sawyer came awake and found the sun well up in the morning sky. The girl's head still rested on his shoulder, and the shoulder was cramped to the point of numbness. He lay there tensely, orienting himself, wondering what had waked him.

He heard it then, the crackle of horses on the rocky trail. He straightened, his movement rousing the girl. Her eyes opened, and she started to speak. Quickly he closed his hand across her mouth.

"They're coming. Don't move unless I tell you."

Chapter Fifteen

CAREFULLY he moved to the natural parapet and peered out through the upthrust stones at the trail below.

He saw the full crew, Kelly in advance, Wilson at his side, the others strung out behind. They rode slowly, their eyes intently searching both sides of the trail.

They halted at the rock slide, and Wilson's deep-throated tones carried up to where Sawyer stood.

"We know they crossed the river. You can't mistake those tracks of Sawyer's bare feet in the sand, and they can't have gotten much farther than this. In fact I'm surprised they got this far. Chances are they're holed up somewhere within a couple of miles, waiting for dark."

"You were right about them backtracking." It was Kelly. "Me, I'd have headed out through the hills north."

"Naw." Wilson shook his head. "It figured. Sawyer's a tenderfoot, and he don't know the country. The only way he knows is the way we came in."

He turned on his horse and called to the men behind him. "Ride on up about two miles. Spread out. Watch for signs where they left the trail, and search anyplace where they could have climbed out of the canyon. We've got to find them. That girl will have the law down on our necks the first chance she gets, and she has Sawyer wrapped around her finger already."

They rode on.

Kelly pulled his horse around. "There's a little draw about a mile back. I'll have a look up there."

"Me, I'm going to try this rock slide." Wilson swung down, dropping the reins over his horse's head so that they trailed the ground. He walked slowly back and forth along the base of the slide, scanning the rubble for marks of human passage.

He chose a place different from the one Sawyer had used and began to climb, working upward unhurriedly, pausing every few feet to study the rocks about him.

His bearing would carry him to Sawyer's left, perhaps a hundred feet away. Sawyer dropped down beside the girl and edged her tight against the foot of the natural wall, so that a searcher would have to stand upon the very rim to look down on them.

He held her thus, warning her with the tenseness of his body, not trusting himself to utter a single word for fear the sound would swell trickishly among the rocks. He felt her small hand reach over and close reassuringly on his. He returned the grip, trying to comfort her, feeling her tremble with the pent-up tension of dread.

They sat motionless, their ears straining, as the slow minutes passed. Once they heard a rock tumble down the slide, and Sawyer guessed it had been dislodged by Wilson's boot. Then quiet settled over the canyon, as if there were no danger within a hundred miles.

The voice came suddenly, out of nowhere, jarring them just when they had begun to believe they might escape detection.

"All right, get up."

Wilson was standing above them, grinning down into their shelter, his gun looking small in the largeness of his hand.

Sawyer rose slowly, then helped the girl to her feet. Her hand clung to his arm as she stared upward.

Wilson was chuckling. "So you thought you could get away. Climb on down."

Without speaking, Sawyer lifted the girl over the rock fence, and in silence they picked their way back down to the trail. Behind them, Wilson took his time in the descent, his gun dangling loosely in his thick fingers.

Had Sawyer been alone, he might have made a try for Wilson's horse, but he knew that the first such move would draw fire from the man above them.

They reached the trail and stopped, waiting for Wilson. He dropped off the last rock and came toward them leisurely.

Without the slightest warning, his free hand snapped out and cuffed Sawyer along the side of the head, hard enough to knock him from his feet. Deliberately Wilson thrust the gun into its holster and stood, his feet wide apart, waiting.

"If you can lick me, you can walk out." There was a note of savage eagerness in the man's heavy voice, as if he could not wait to get his huge hands on Sawyer.

"Don't." It was the girl's voice. "For God's sake, Marc, don't. He'll kill you."

Wilson laughed at her, and as he turned his head Sawyer jumped from his hands and knees in a charging leap that carried him across the five feet that separated them, driving his shoulder hard into the big man's stomach. Surprise, plus the weight behind the shoulder, jarred Wilson over backward. He crashed heavily to the ground with Sawyer on top of him.

For an instant the jar had knocked the wind out of Wilson, and Sawyer managed to sit up on the big chest, to drive a right to the side of the huge head.

Instead of knocking him out, the blow seemed to revive Wilson. He suddenly arched his great body like a bucking horse and threw Sawyer bodily into the air. Then he rolled, coming onto his hands and knees, and pounced on the smaller man as Sawyer fell to the ground.

They rolled in each other's arms, bumping across the stony trail, crashing hard enough against a high rock to break Wilson's bear hug.

Sawyer rolled away and struggled to his feet, his tortured lungs sucking greedily at the thin mountain air, his ribs aching from Wilson's crushing hold.

Through a red haze he watched Wilson rise and stand for an instant shaking himself, watched him start forward, the bullet head on its thick neck outthrust like an angry turtle looking for something to snap at, the arms extended, the hands clawlike, clutching for their victim.

Wilson lunged in, trying to wrap his arms again about the slighter figure. This time Sawyer sidestepped, avoiding the hug, and smashed his knuckles full into the red face.

The blow stopped Wilson's charge but failed to put him down. He shook his head like a tortured bull, and Sawyer hit him a second time, a right flush to the jaw, the impact so hard that it numbed Sawyer's arm. Still Wilson did not fall. He came on as relentlessly as death, crowding Sawyer into a corner between two enormous standing rocks.

Sawyer saw the trap too late. He tried to duck aside, and Wilson hit him with a looping sweep that knocked him back against the rock mercilessly.

Shaken and desperate, he charged, only to be met by a right to his head and a crushing left to his stomach, to have the wind pile-driven entirely out of him.

He fell down, twisted into a knot, desperately sick.

Wilson blew hot air from the bellows of his lungs. Then with a deliberateness masking the rage that gripped him, the giant reached down with his left hand, caught a handful of Sawyer's hair, and calmly lifted him upright. With a deep-felt pleasure he plunged his free fist into Sawyer's partly open mouth.

Blood welled from Sawyer's lips. The girl, who had stood horrified, now ran in and, wrapping herself about Wilson's arm, tried to wrestle him back.

"Stop it, stop it. You'll kill him."

Wilson flung the arm away in a sweeping backward motion that swatted her from her feet.

Sawyer struck weakly at the wide rib cage, with no more effect than if his fists were filled with feathers. Wilson hit him again, still holding the tight grip on his hair, hanging his victim upright for the punishment he so enjoyed giving.

The girl came up slowly. Through the red fog that screened his eyes, Sawyer saw her rise. He knew he was going to die. The thought oozed through his mind, now functioning at less than half speed. He was certain now that Wilson meant to kill him, that there was a sadistic streak in the big outlaw that he normally kept under control but that fed on violence.

Sawyer reached up, trying to loosen the heavy fingers that still gripped his hair, threatening to pull it out by the roots with each succeeding blow.

He caught the middle finger, and with the last of his strength bent it backward until the bone snapped.

With a cry of rage Wilson picked him up and tossed him clear across the trail. Then vindictively the outlaw pulled out his gun with his uninjured hand and leveled it at the semiconscious Sawyer.

"Stop it." Joel Kelly had ridden around the shoulder of the rock slide. "Stop it."

Wilson turned, fury twisting his big face until it was hardly recognizable.

"The bastard broke my finger. I'll blow his fool head off."

"No." Joel Kelly's gun was in his hand. His voice was chill, his eyes icy. "Put that away, or I'll shoot it out of your hand."

To Sawyer the words seemed to come from a long distance. He tried to open his eyes, but the lids felt weighted with lead.

He knew vaguely that he owed his life to Joel Kelly, but at the moment that did not register as important. He hardly heard Wilson's snarling protest, or Kelly's sharp reply.

"We need him, you fool. Who else have we got to send into Spokane after Tupper? When this job is finished you can have him. I don't care what happens to the rat. Now get him on your horse while I round up the rest of the crew. If you kill him while I'm gone, I'll cut you into small pieces."

He pulled his horse about and rode on up the trail, in utter confidence that his orders would be obeyed. Wilson stared after him.

The girl began to crawl toward where Sawyer lay. Wilson caught her up and flung her violently across the trail and against the rocks. She crumpled to the ground.

"You bitch. If it hadn't been for you, none of this would have happened."

He stalked toward Sawyer and stood staring down at the

semiconscious man. Then, with the deliberation with which he did most things, he brought up his right boot and kicked Sawyer under the chin as hard as he could.

Sawyer's head snapped back with nearly enough force to break his neck. Wilson viewed his work and some of the rage drained from his face. Its contortion was replaced by a self-satisfied grin.

"I'll bet he doesn't try something again real soon."

He stooped, and without effort lifted Sawyer's inert body and slung it like a soft sack across the saddle of his horse.

He paid no attention to the girl. Instead he stood examining his broken finger, grimacing as he tried to force the bone back into place.

He was still working on the finger when Kelly rode up with the crew.

Kelly swung down. Ignoring his sister, he went directly to Wilson. He took the big man's hand, studied the finger. Without a word he dropped it, found two small sticks, and set the bone and bound it tightly in place between the improvised splints.

He turned then to stare thoughtfully at Sawyer. Finally he nodded at the silent Wilson.

"For beating him up you get to walk back to the river. Go ahead. Lead the horse."

Almost meekly the huge man moved to obey. The killer instinct, which had held him in its grip throughout the course of the fight, was entirely washed away.

He crossed over and picked up the reins. Kelly glanced at his sister.

"Would you rather ride with me or walk?"

The look she gave him was one of absolute contempt.

"I'd rather walk," she said, and started up the trail.

Chapter Sixteen

SAWYER regained consciousness slowly. It was after dark when he became aware that they had returned to the campsite from which he and the girl had fled. He opened his eyes, looking around uncertainly.

To the right, a dozen feet away, a fire burned, and he could see the dark, moving shapes of men against the dancing light.

The girl sat at his side, hunched against the cold of the downdraft, trying to break the wind with her small body, to keep it from beating upon his blanket-wrapped body.

He stirred, and a small groan escaped unknown from his lips. At once she bent over him. Her fingers were cool and reassuring against his hot forehead, her voice a soft whisper that did not carry as far as the fire.

"Marc, Marc."

He lay still, fully conscious now, the aches of his many bruises flooding through him.

"Yes?"

He did not know how weak his answer was. He only knew that he seemed to have to summon the word from a great distance.

"You . . . you want some coffee?" She could think of nothing else to say.

He managed to nod, and the resulting pain in his stiffened neck made him cry out.

She rose and, conscious that her brother and his followers

watched, moved to the fire and half filled a tin cup from the
blackened, simmering pot.

She cooled it with water from the creek, and carried it back.
Gently she raised his head to let him sip painfully from the
battered cup.

The warm liquid ran down him in a comforting wave. Afterward he slept, his exhausted body relaxing as it had not done
before.

He did not know that the girl sat there through the
night, cradling his head on her lap. He did not know that
twice during the dark hours Kelly came to look at him and
she ordered him away.

The following day was pure torture. Wilson routed them
out early, and they were on the trail by daylight. Kelly rode
in front, then Sawyer with the girl at his side. After them
trailed Wilson and the crew, and the big man took a fiendish
delight in pushing the gait, especially when the going was
roughest.

They made a new camp after dark, and Sawyer fell as he
stepped from his horse. By the next morning the native
strength of his muscular body had reasserted itself, and the
second day was far easier.

They crossed the pass, and worked steadily down the
western slope. Sawyer had no idea how far they had come or
how far there was yet to go, but he was not surprised when
Kelly pulled alongside his horse and made a sweeping gesture
ahead. Far below wound the thread of the Spokane River.

The town of Spokane Falls, some fifteen years old, had
grown more rapidly than any other center of the inland
empire, which lay sheltered on the west by the Cascades
and on the east by the high, wicked crags of the Rockies.

The town sprawled on both sides of the rushing river from
which it took its name. The shipping point for the mines, the
ranches, and the farmers of the country, it was a roaring,
brawling town whose sidewalks shook to the pound of cowboy boots, of miners' shoes, and to the tread of railroad men.

Kelly twisted in his saddle and faced Sawyer squarely,
thoughtfully.

"You're going to ride in," he said. "I don't dare send one of the others. They might be recognized. You're going to find Tupper, and you'll tell him that we want fifty thousand dollars by tomorrow night or he won't live out the week."

"What if he laughs at me? What if he calls in the sheriff?"

Kelly's face was hawklike in its viciousness. "He won't do that. As long as he knows I'm loose, as long as he realizes I'm free to strike, he won't dare to cross me. He knows me, and he knows what happens to people who cross me."

Sawyer turned to the girl, on his other side, then around, looking into the faces of the men.

"Supposing he delivers the money and then tells the law you're still in this part of the country?"

"He won't. You're going to make him deliver the money himself, and we won't turn him loose until we get to the Canadian border."

Sawyer nodded slowly.

Kelly sounded more pleasant than he had in days.

"Don't make any slips. If you do, you won't have a girl when you come back. Now get moving."

Sawyer turned again to Virginia, surprising the tight look of hopelessness on her small face. He reached across and squeezed her hand. Then without a word he put his horse down the hill and rode the three miles between the crew and the town.

He rode absently, his mind busy studying the possible courses of action open to him. He could get in touch with Paul Chum, and the railroader would blanket the country with men to make certain that Kelly did not again escape.

But what would happen to Virginia?

On the other hand, if he went into town without contacting Chum and the railroader saw him, there would be explanations he could not make.

He rode on in, past the railroad yards, to stable his horse at a livery backing up on the surging river.

It was nearly dark when he came again to the street and turned up the dusty ribbon of First, and moved along it to the town's largest saloon.

The room was crowded with the before-supper trade, and he looked carefully over the heads to assure himself that Chum was not present.

He had no fear of running into Bob Holt. The detective was still far to the east, leading the search for the escaped outlaws. The last place anyone would look for Joel Kelly and his murderers was in Spokane Falls.

He found a place at the bar and had his first drink in days, feeling the warmth of the raw whiskey burn through his tired body. The bartender glanced at him curiously, for his face still bore the marks and bruises put there by Wilson's clubbing fists, but after catching Sawyer's eyes the man checked the comment that had sprung to his lips.

Sawyer shoved his empty glass back across the counter and watched the man refill it.

"Would you know where Tupper the banker lives?"

His question was low-voiced. It hardly carried to the bartender's ears above the babble that rode like a smothering cloud over the smoke-filled room.

The man looked at him again, then nodded. "It's a white house with a picket fence, about four blocks out Second. You can't miss it. It's beside Fowler's General Store."

Sawyer nodded his thanks, lifted his second drink to his lips, and downed it slowly. There was a cut inside his right cheek where Wilson's knuckles had driven the flesh against his teeth. The whiskey seared it, making him wince.

He raised his eyes and saw the calendar above the bartender's head. It was September third, five long months since he had first made contact with Joel Kelly.

He wondered, as he paid for the drinks and turned away, if there would ever be an end, if the bandit would ever be brought to justice for his crimes.

He found the house without difficulty. He pushed open the gate in the neat picket fence and threaded his way over the boardwalk to the low porch.

A lamp burned in the front room, its light laying a path for him across the porch. He came up the two steps, and his knuckles made a hollow sound on the front door as he knocked.

Inside, there was a stir, a murmur of voices, a man's and a woman's. Sawyer had not entertained the possibility that Tupper might be married, that there might be a woman involved.

The thought had barely touched his mind when the door opened and Tupper stood staring out at him.

The surprise in the banker's face was a physical thing. It was replaced almost at once by fear, and his voice had a breathless quality as he said, "Where'd you come from?"

Sawyer knew guilt when he saw it, and he was certain now that this man was responsible for the substitution of the washers in the pay load. Whatever compassion he had had for the banker washed away.

From the lighted room beyond a woman's voice called. "Who is it, Al?"

"No one you know." The man's tone showed strain in spite of his effort to steady it, and the woman went on with a note of alarm, "Al, what is it?"

"Just a little business," he told her. "I'll be back in a few minutes."

He stepped onto the porch, pulling the door closed behind him. Taking Sawyer's arm, he led him down from the porch and out along the walk to the fence.

Behind them the door opened again, and a gaunt woman peered into the dark yard.

"Al?"

"It's all right." His voice roughened with emotion. "Go to bed. I'll explain later."

She hesitated, framed in the bright doorway. Then, reluctantly, she shut the door and left the two men alone in the night.

Tupper was marshaling his thoughts. He took a long breath before he said, "What do you want?"

Sawyer's tone was flat, final.

"The money."

He heard a slight wheeze as the banker sucked in air.

"I don't know what you're talking about."

Sawyer reached out, and his hand closed on Tupper's arm with such force that Tupper cried out sharply.

"Don't play games."

He twisted the arm a little to emphasize his meaning.

"Washers don't make a very good payroll. How would you have explained them to the railroad if we hadn't held up the train?"

He could not see plainly enough to be certain, but he thought that Tupper ran a nervous tongue around the circle of his dry lips.

"You can't prove anything."

Sawyer's laugh was short and without mirth. "Since when does Kelly need to prove anything? He doesn't go into court before he uses a gun."

The banker had recovered his control.

"Don't try to frighten me by using Kelly's name. If he's smart, he's already in Canada. The country is up in arms after that massacre. They've even ordered out the cavalry to help catch him."

"That's where you're wrong." Sawyer turned and pointed toward the hills east of town. "Kelly's waiting up there for us to bring the money, and he won't wait too long. You've got until tomorrow night."

The words struck the banker with the force of a blow. He said without conviction, "I don't believe you."

Sawyer sounded indifferent. "Your business. Either Kelly has that fifty thousand by tomorrow night or you're dead. It's your choice."

"But where could I get that kind of money?"

"Your problem. What did you do with the money that was supposed to be in the pay car? Drag it out of where you hid it."

The man's groan was agonized. "There isn't any money. I was short nearly that amount at the bank. Why else do you think I did it? I was desperate."

Sawyer could only stare at him. He did not know whether to believe the banker. There was no doubt that Tupper was tricky. This could be an excuse to avoid handing over the stolen money. But if it was true, what happened now? What happened to Virginia Kelly, waiting up in the hills with the outlaws, waiting for him to come and rescue her?

If he went back to Kelly with that story, there was no guessing what the man would do, what would happen to the girl and to himself.

He might force the banker to accompany him, to tell the story to Kelly, but how could he accomplish even this? Kelly had not returned his gun, and he was certain Tupper would not leave town unless he was forced to.

It was obvious the man was scared. It showed in the way he twisted around, like a mouse caught in a corner, searching for a route of escape.

He took a step backward in retreat toward the house, and Sawyer caught his arm. He did not know what he intended to do. He did not expect Tupper to reach for a gun. It had not occurred to him that the man went armed in his own home.

But Tupper used his free hand to try to drag a weapon clear of his coat pocket.

Sawyer hit him full on the jaw and watched the man drop. He stooped swiftly to recover the gun. It was a thirty-eight with a short barrel, but the feel of the smooth stock plates in his palm was cool and reassuring.

He stood, waiting for the man on the ground to stir, to sit up groggily.

"On your feet."

Tupper tried twice before he made it. He stumbled around, rubbing his chin where Sawyer's knuckles had cracked against the bone, shaking his head to clear it.

Sawyer said quietly, "Now you and I are going to walk down to the livery, get some horses, and ride out and talk to Kelly. Don't try to duck it. I'll shoot you the first wrong move you make."

The man's voice was shaky. "I've got to tell my wife."

Sawyer had forgotten the wife. He hesitated, then nodded.

He did not want Tupper's wife raising the town in search of her husband.

"All right. Walk back up onto the porch, open the door, and call to her that you have to ride out to see a man on business and that you don't know when you'll be back. Don't try to go inside the house, or I'll shoot you in the back."

He watched the banker turn slowly, mount the two steps, cross the porch, and open the door. Sawyer did not follow up the steps, but contented himself with remaining in the shadows, the gun in his hand.

He heard Tupper call to his wife, "A deal has come up. I have to ride out and see about it."

He heard her complaining answer. "That's all you ever think of, work, work, work. One of these times when you go out at night I won't be home when you come back."

It crossed Sawyer's mind that the husband might not be coming back, but he had no sympathy for Tupper. The man was an even sorrier specimen than he had thought. Not only had he served as an agent for the outlaws, but he had also stolen from his own bank.

In disgust he watched the man close the door and come back to his side. They walked again to the gate, without speaking. Once on the sidewalk, where he was certain his words would not carry to the house, Tupper said in a low voice, "If I gave you five thousand dollars, would you let me ride out of town, west?"

"Sorry."

The man's voice broke. "Kelly will kill me. I know he will. You might as well shoot me now."

"Keep walking."

They moved on in silence. Sawyer had thrust the gun into his side coat pocket, but he kept his hand on it. He wondered whether he could bring himself to shoot the man down if, driven by desperation, Tupper tried to run. And if Tupper did get away, he wondered how he would explain to Joel Kelly.

But Tupper lacked the courage to even try. Sawyer kept crowding him, hurrying him toward the livery.

They came into the wide runway, with its warm smells of fresh hay and grain, and found the barn man forking bedding into one of the box stalls.

He glanced at them, and Sawyer said, "My horse, and one for Mr. Tupper."

Curiosity showed in the barn man's eyes. "Be out long, Mr. Tupper?"

Sawyer felt the man at his side stiffen. If Tupper ever meant to make a break, this was his best chance. Sawyer said quickly, "Not too long. He's going to show me a ranch."

The barn man went away. Tupper ran his tongue tip around his lips. In the light from the lantern hanging against the post his face had a green cast, and when the horses were led out he mounted with the heaviness of a man climbing to the scaffold.

They rode out, Tupper in the lead, Sawyer only a pace behind, past the crowded saloons, past people moving along the sidewalk, past the dark building of the bank. They turned to parallel the railroad, leaving the town behind, and started up the thin trail that wound through the hills.

They had traveled a good two miles, the country around them turned by the moon into a silver, ghostlike world. As they rounded a small bend, a big figure suddenly loomed before them and Jumbo Wilson's leaden voice cut through the night.

"Hold up."

Tupper's horse stopped automatically. Sawyer almost rode into him. Behind Wilson half a dozen figures materialized out of the brush, and Sawyer caught a flash of the girl's white face as she came toward him, herded by her brother. Before he could speak to her Kelly's voice whipped out, "The money? Did you bring the money?"

Chapter Seventeen

"THERE isn't any money."

The words burst from Tupper, exploded by the panic that filled him.

"You've got to understand, Joel. I didn't take any money out of those pay sacks. I've been short in my accounts for years, juggling one bookkeeping entry against another. This was my only chance to get even."

Kelly rode forward until his knee almost touched the banker's. He stared at the huddled figure in incredulous silence. Then he stood up in his stirrups and deliberately drove his fist into Tupper's face.

The blow knocked the banker from his horse. He fell and rolled beneath Sawyer's horse, and the animal reared. Only by inches did the descending hoofs miss crushing the fallen man, as Sawyer brought the animal under quick control.

Wilson was out of his saddle in an instant. He stooped, caught Tupper's shoulder in one big hand, and jerked the groggy man to his feet, shaking him as if he were made of rags.

Kelly spoke sharply, and Wilson quit shaking Tupper but without releasing his grip on the man's shoulders. Kelly swung down leisurely, handing his reins to Sawyer. He stood spread-legged, his thumbs hooked in his gun belt.

"So you've been stealing money from your bank, and you set me up as the fall guy to cover your operations."

Tupper stared at the ground.

"It was you who thought up the holdup. You wrote me about the delayed payroll. It was a nice try, Tupper. I should hang you to a tree."

It was plain from Tupper's face that he expected exactly this to happen.

"So you put the washers in the pay sacks and expected the holdup to cover you. I wish we hadn't stopped that train. I wish the railroad would get you, the way you deserve."

Had Sawyer been less worried about the girl, he would have counted the last words amusing. The idea of Joel Kelly lecturing anyone on honesty was laughable.

"How much money have you got left in that bank?"

Tupper glanced up at Kelly, and Sawyer sensed the hope that coursed through the man.

"We had something like thirty thousand in cash at closing tonight."

"Fine. We're riding in to get it."

The men behind Kelly stirred uneasily. They did not relish the idea of venturing into Spokane at this time, when the whole country was roused against them.

Sawyer said quietly, "I did what you asked. I brought Tupper to you. How about letting me ride out with your sister as you promised?"

Kelly did not even look at him. "No. She'd head for the first sheriff. I'll turn her loose as soon as we get to Canada. Where you go from there is your business."

The ride down into Spokane was leisurely. Neither Kelly nor Wilson pushed the pace. When they drew into the town most of the people had deserted the streets and most of the saloons were closed.

Sawyer guessed it was nearing morning. The girl was at his side, riding silently. She had not spoken since they had dropped out of the hills.

Kelly rode in the lead, very erect in his saddle. The derby

hat, which always struck Sawyer as being out of place, was cocked at a forward angle on his handsome head.

A deferential pace behind, subdued, hunched in his saddle as if the weight of the thoughts he carried with him was too much, Tupper was sunk in utter silence.

Apparently he had given up all hope of escape. Apparently he even welcomed the idea of Kelly cleaning out the bank. Perhaps his shortages were larger than he had admitted, too large to cover with the phony payroll.

They followed the street to the bank corner, turned it, and halted. Kelly took a long look in both directions, and then led the way into the alley behind the dark building and stepped down before the rear door.

"Jeff, you stay with the horses. Frank, keep an eye on my sister. If she tries to make a sound or to get away, rap her head with your gun, and I don't care how hard you hit her. The rest of you stand watch on the street. Jumbo, you and Sawyer come on inside with me."

Sawyer swore softly. He had hoped he and the girl might have a chance to make a break in the darkness of the alley. He swung down, and as he passed her, he touched her hand in reassurance.

Then he trailed Tupper and Kelly into the bank, very conscious that Wilson followed him.

The long room was in deep shadow, its only light the reflection of the suffused glow of moonlight in the street that filtered through the front windows.

Now that they were inside, Tupper's agitation returned. Kelly motioned with his hand, and Wilson ghosted across to take up a post beside the glass front of the bank.

Tupper's whisper was hoarse. "I'll have to have some light to work the combination."

Kelly grunted. "What about the street?"

Wilson's voice rumbled back to them in a growling whisper. "No one in sight."

Kelly found a lamp on the counter, lifted the chimney, and lit the wick. He turned the flame low as he carried the lamp to Tupper's side. He crouched next to him before the looming safe.

Sawyer watched them, hungry to touch the gun in his coat pocket. No one had thought to search him after he took Tupper into the hills.

He could use it. He could shoot Kelly in the back before the bandit knew what was happening. But Wilson was behind him. The first move he made would bring death from the big lieutenant.

He shifted his position, intending to edge toward the windows to a spot where he could get the drop on both men, but Kelly turned his head.

"What are you doing?"

Sawyer shrugged. "Wilson can't watch both ends of the street at once." His facial bruises had not yet healed, and it hurt him to talk.

"Stay where you are." Kelly was again suspicious, and he kept jerking his head to glance back at Sawyer. After some minutes he swore irritably at Tupper. "Stop stalling and get that safe open."

The banker spun the combination feverishly, then began to work the series of numbers again.

"I'm trying. I made a mistake somewhere."

The minutes dragged like hours. Wilson's voice came suddenly.

"Kill the light. Someone's coming."

Kelly blew out the light and was on his feet in an instant, cat-footing to Sawyer's side.

His whisper had the thrust of a hot knife blade. "If you make a sound . . ." The barrel of his gun rammed into Sawyer's ribs.

They stood tense, motionless.

Outside, they could hear the rasp of a man's boots on the hollow wooden sidewalk. He stumbled along the street, passing the empty windows of the bank without even glancing at them. He cut diagonally across the intersection and disappeared into the shadows of the side street.

The pressure of Kelly's gun was withdrawn from Sawyer's ribs, and the leader called softly to Wilson, "All clear?"

"Can't see nobody else."

Kelly went back, relighted the lamp, and squatted again at Tupper's side. The banker showed him a face streaked with nervous sweat. Kelly's voice was harsh.

"Get that safe open, or I'll have Jumbo blow it."

The man nodded, and his shaking hand again went to the dial. He twisted right, left, right, left. One by one the tumblers fell into place. He turned the handle and pulled open the ponderous door.

Behind Sawyer, Wilson drew his breath in noisy satisfaction.

Kelly shoved Tupper aside, and the man lost his balance and sprawled on the floor. Kelly took no notice. He set the lamp down beside him and began dragging out the heavy sacks of silver and gold.

There was very little paper. The West still mistrusted anything but hard money, remembering too vividly the shinplasters of the postwar years.

Kelly made no effort to count the sacks. He continued pulling them out, stacking them on the floor beside the safe, saying across his shoulder, "Sawyer, call in a couple of the boys, and we'll get this stuff in the saddlebags."

Sawyer moved past him toward the rear entrance, every nerve alert. He knew that if he was ever to make a break, it had to be now. Once they were in the saddle, once they were riding for the border, Kelly would watch him and the girl like a hawk.

He reached the door and stepped outside, pausing to readjust his eyes to the gloom. He located the men scattered along the alley, one at the corner watching the side street, one at the other end of the block, one holding the horses, and one guarding Virginia Kelly.

He called softly. His hand was in his pocket, gripping the gun hard. He meant to shoot his way out if necessary, but it would be far better if he could get the girl in the clear before the firing started.

The two riders from the alley's ends came swiftly toward him, one saying in an excited tone, "Trouble?"

"No trouble. Kelly wants you all inside to help carry out the money."

The man laughed. "That's the job I like." The ill-humor with which he had regarded Sawyer had faded from his voice. The prospect of the golden hoard inside had wiped away the doubts and suspicions he had harbored.

The man holding the horses whispered, "How many of us?"

"All of you. I'll take care of the horses."

"Not me." It was the guard beside the girl. "Joel told me to watch her."

"Not you," Sawyer agreed at once. "You're to stay here." He stepped across and held out his free hand for the reins held by the hostler. The man put them into his palm.

The horses stood bunched, their heads close together, their rumps spread out in a fanlike half-circle, motionless. They were too well-trained to be restless, and they had traveled a long way.

Sawyer saw the three men swallowed by the bank doorway and knew that he must move at once. Soon the outlaw chief would realize that Sawyer and the girl were in the alley with a single guard.

He eased the gun from his pocket, dropped the reins, and took three quick steps. He hoped to reach the man and swing the gun barrel down on his head before the other guessed his intent, but the guard had been peering intently at him in the darkness ever since the others had started into the building.

He dropped the reins of the girl's horse and went for his gun.

Marc Sawyer shot him in the stomach.

He was moving even as the man fell, even as his shot echoed and re-echoed in the narrow confines of the alley. He snatched up the gun that had dropped from the guard's nerveless hand and thrust it at Virginia Kelly.

"Get out of here, quick. Get help."

With his hat he struck the horse on the rump and saw it

jump into motion. Then he turned and charged the bunched animals, flailing his arms, shouting at them as he came.

They reared away, milling about, bumping into each other, as they jostled for passageway down the alley.

He watched them go with a surge of relief. Whatever happened now, Kelly and his men were on foot. They would find it hard to escape from the town without mounts.

He swung again, in time to see Kelly appear in the half light of the bank doorway. He threw his shot, and it stung against the frame within an inch of Kelly's head, making the outlaw duck back quickly into the shelter of the bank.

Sawyer's strategy was to pen the men inside the building as long as possible, but he was acutely conscious that he had fired two shots, that only four remained in the cylinder, and that the cartridges in his belt would not fit the smaller gun.

The smart thing would be to retreat down the alley. He chose, instead, to creep forward toward the still open doorway. He reached the bank's rear wall and worked along it, his gun ready.

No head appeared, and he gained the jamb and peered around it to see Wilson and two others slip through the front entrance.

The remaining crew, including Kelly, were hastily hefting up the sacks, as if they meant to follow Wilson.

Deliberately Sawyer raised his gun and aimed at Kelly, doing something he had never before done, shooting at a man who was not directly threatening him.

Even as he fired, Kelly bent over to pick up a sack of money, and the bullet cut above him, smashing the lamp upon the counter, flinging burning oil across the room, showering the drapes on the side windows.

The cloth was aflame in an instant, the blaze fed by the sprayed oil.

Had any of the men in the bank cared to, they could have checked the flames before they ate into the dried boards of the building wall.

But not even Tupper made an attempt to halt the growing

fire—a fire that was to burn for two days and destroy most of the business section.

Sawyer shot again, this time hitting Kelly in the shoulder. Then the outlaws' bullets drove him back into the alley, splintering the doorframe against which he had braced himself.

He spun out, in time to see Wilson's massive figure loom at the juncture of alley and side street, to hear the shots as the big man cut down on him.

One bullet whispered through the cloth of his coat, tugging at it without breaking his skin. Then Wilson was joined by the second man, and both were firing.

Sawyer did not return the shots. He had two bullets left.

Across the alley stretched a fence, shoulder-high. He covered the rutted ground in three long leaps, caught the top board, and hurled himself over it, falling heavily on one shoulder as he came down.

He lay for a minute, the wind partially knocked out of him—and thereby probably saved his life. Above him, Wilson's bullets cut a swath across the fence, and a moment later three more guns joined in the barrage as Kelly's group tumbled out of the bank.

Sawyer rolled away. He heard their voices calling back and forth in the alley, and then the sound of running feet as someone rushed at the fence.

He was in a yard behind a store, the baked, bare ground littered with piles of old lumber and crating. He had found shelter behind one of these piles by the time a man's head appeared over the top of the fence, silhouetted against the red glow of the burning bank. Already the alley was bathed in its hot brilliance.

But the yard in which Sawyer crouched was still shadowed, and the man called nervously, "I can't see him."

"Get over and dig him out," Wilson's voice was weighted and thick with anger. "The fink, I'll break every bone in his body."

"Let him go." It was Kelly. "Let's get this gold out of here before the whole town shows up. We've got to get horses."

"Fat chance we've got."

"We'll get them." Kelly was master of himself and the situation. "Just get off this block, and no one will pay any attention to us. They'll be too damn busy fighting the fire."

The outlaw's head dropped behind the fence, and Sawyer heard the men's scuffing feet move hastily down the alley.

He rose. He had no intention of letting Kelly escape now. He wondered why no one had arrived at the fire. The barrage of shots certainly had wakened the town. And then he realized that it had been only short minutes since Virginia Kelly drove away, since he stampeded the horses down the alley.

He stood listening, hearing men shouting somewhere out on the street in front of the bank. He moved toward the fence and lifted himself over it.

He almost stepped on Jumbo Wilson as he dropped down. The huge man was crouched there like a gigantic spider waiting for a fly to fall into its clutch.

Chapter Eighteen

WILSON rose as Sawyer dropped to his side. One big arm shot out to lock about Sawyer's throat, pulling his head back until his neck was so taut he could not breathe.

"Got you."

The voice was buttery with satisfaction.

"Figured you were still there. Figured you'd come wandering out as soon as you thought we'd gone."

His free hand was going over Sawyer's pockets as he talked. He found the gun, pulled it out, and tossed it casually

over the fence. Then he released his grip on Sawyer's throat
and locked his big arm through Marc's.

"Try something now, and I'll break your neck right here."

Sawyer was surprised to still be alive. Wilson turned, not
in the direction Kelly and the others had gone, but toward
the street beside the bank. They came out of the alley, and
his strategy was at once apparent.

Already the space before the burning building was thronged,
and as they appeared one of the volunteer fire companies
dashed up, shouting for passage through the crowd.

In the confusion no one noticed their arrival, and they
began working their way up the street.

The three buildings above the bank were now ablaze, and
the wind from the west was driving the fire forward in an
ever-increasing blast.

The whole district was a jumble of sound, the crowd growing with each passing second, and Sawyer realized that Kelly
had been right: if they found horses, the outlaws could ride
out unchallenged, to all purposes unnoticed.

They pushed on up the street. Twice Sawyer tried to wrench
free when he thought that Wilson had relaxed his grip,
and twice he nearly had his arm jerked from its socket.

The man's strength was incredible. Sawyer saw then that
even in this crowd he was an utter captive, that were he to
call for help, Wilson would kill him before anyone could
separate them.

The milling mob thinned as they drew farther from the
fire, although people still passed them, running toward the
holocaust, which was spreading hungrily along the block.
By the time they reached the livery that part of the town
was deserted.

Inside the runway they found Kelly's men hurriedly sad-
dling. The hostler was nowhere in sight, and Sawyer guessed
that he had already joined the firefighters.

There was a sudden explosion from the direction of the
bank. Either they were dynamiting buildings in an effort
to halt the inferno or the fire had reached a powder storage
in one of the mining-supply houses.

Sawyer had no time to think about this, for Kelly swung around as they came in, gaping at him, saying harshly, "Why'd you bring him along?"

Wilson still gripped Sawyer's arm. "Didn't have time to kill him. Someone might have spotted us in the alley, and there was too much of a crowd on the street."

"All right, get a horse and let's ride."

"No hurry. That bunch at the fire will be busy for hours." He shook his victim like a terrier. "I hate double-crossers. I'm going to break your nose and both arms and both legs." He held up the hand with the center finger Sawyer had snapped. "And then I'm going to break every damn finger you've got. When I get through you'll pray for me to shoot you. Maybe I will, maybe I won't."

There was a box stall in the rear corner, its heavy plank sides as high as a man's head. Wilson shoved Sawyer toward it, pulled open the gate, and pushed him inside with such force that Sawyer stumbled in the thick straw and fell headlong, his arms extended.

Under one arm he felt a stick buried in the straw. He lay there, working his fingers around it. Then slowly he came up to his hands and knees, without pulling the round handle from its bedding of straw.

He twisted his head and saw that Wilson had stepped into the stall, had closed the gate behind him, and now stood, his legs wide apart, his big hands outthrust greedily as if he could not wait for the pleasure of closing them around the smaller man's throat.

Sawyer got his feet under him and came up swiftly, realizing with a burst of hope that he held a three-tined hay fork.

He swung then to confront Wilson, the fork thrust out before him like a spear.

Wilson saw the fork, the glitter in Sawyer's eyes, and did not hesitate. He knew that he could not ward off the sharp, needlelike points with his arm, that Sawyer would impale him on the prongs.

He could not retreat. The gate behind him was shut, and he would have to jump sideways to swing it open past his thick body. He had no time to call for help. Kelly and the crew had already led the saddled horses into the road.

He went for his gun. His big hand swept down, the curling fingers hooking around the worn stock, and lifted it from the leather holster in a single swinging gesture as rapid as anything Sawyer had ever seen.

But even as Wilson started to draw, Sawyer had thrown himself forward, both hands tight on the fork handle, but not aiming for the stomach.

The center prong struck the wide wrist as it lifted the gun and ran through it, pushing Wilson backward. The fork dug its way into the hard wood of the gate, pinning him there, and the gun dropped from suddenly limp fingers.

A harsh, startled cry burst from Wilson's lips. For a moment he was too dazed to move, then he heaved, heedless of the pain, to tear himself free of the pinioning tines.

The fork came loose just as Sawyer hit him squarely on the jaw. He brought the blow up from knee-level, putting everything he had into it.

He felt his knuckle split, and the pain that lanced up his arm clear to his shoulder staggered him.

His blow had snapped Wilson's head back against the upper edge of the gate, and the big man shook it groggily, trying to clear it, trying to force his eyes back into focus.

Then, ignoring the fact that his wrist had been one-third severed by the fork, that the center finger of his other hand was broken, Wilson lowered his head and sprang forward, trying to use his head and the drive of his legs as a ram to butt Sawyer from his feet.

Sawyer sidestepped, sticking out his leg, and Wilson stumbled over it. As the big man fell past him, Sawyer chopped down at the brute neck with the rigid edge of his hand.

Wilson dropped on his face. Sawyer kicked him twice in the side. Then he spun and jumped for the big man's fallen gun.

He bent over. His fingers closed around the weapon.

Wilson tackled him from behind, flattening them both in the straw, with Wilson on top.

The enormous, injured hands closed on Sawyer's neck, and despite the pain that coursed through the arms, the great fingers squeezed until Sawyer felt that his Adam's apple had collapsed.

Sawyer writhed and rolled, fighting to break the grip while he still had strength. He tore free, kicking at the big man, and Wilson made yet another grab for him.

This time the broken hand slid down his arm, clutching at Sawyer's wrist, twisting, straining to force Sawyer to drop the gun.

Sawyer used the last of his waning strength to turn the heavy barrel against Wilson's side. He pulled the trigger twice, the explosions muffled by the outlaw's thick sheep-lined coat.

Jumbo Wilson died without a sound, died partly in Sawyer's arms, and Sawyer was forced to wrestle the inert weight from his legs in order to rise.

He staggered up. His neck felt broken in several places. He pulled open the gate and lurched into the barn runway.

A shot snapped at him from the front doorway. The bullet cut wood from the post beside his head. He knocked the lighted lantern from its hanging place with a single shot, and it crashed to the ground. Oil spilled on the splintered wood, yet somehow failed to ignite.

Outside, the eastern sky was pale, but the rising light did not penetrate the shadows of the long runway.

Sawyer could hear Kelly shouting orders for his men to mount, and he ran forward clumsily, ignoring the danger to himself. He reached the entrance in time to see the crew swing up into their saddles. He shot at Kelly and missed, hitting the horse that danced between them.

The horse reared, unseating its startled rider, and jarred Kelly's mount, spinning it halfway round, so that he was unable to return Sawyer's shot.

Kelly fought to keep his seat. Three of his riders cut down on Sawyer, and one shot caught him in the leg, another in the left arm.

Sawyer sat down abruptly in the dust, and from that position returned their fire, squeezing the trigger before the hammer fell on an empty cartridge.

His first bullet dropped a man from the saddle. His second ripped the derby hat from Kelly's head.

The other riders were swinging away, racing along the street toward safety, but not Kelly. Kelly had his horse under control now and was steadying the jumpy animal with his free hand.

He realized that Sawyer's gun was empty and rode forward very slowly toward the sitting man. Very deliberately he raised his gun to take aim.

Sawyer sat, powerless to move, helpless to escape the reach of the gun that would kill him. He closed his eyes. Not that he feared to meet death, but he could not watch the smirk of self-satisfied triumph that lighted Kelly's handsome face.

He had failed.

The shot was sharp, whiplike in intensity.

Unconsciously his body tensed against the shock of the homing bullet. It did not come.

Sawyer opened his eyes to stare in disbelief at Kelly, now slumping forward in his saddle, now slipping sidewise as a lifeless foot lost the stirrup, now tumbling to the ground almost at Sawyer's feet.

Virginia Kelly rode warily around the corner of the building. The gun in her hand still smoked, and her face was grim and very white in the glow of morning.

She swung down, holding the weapon at ready, as if she was not yet certain that her brother was no longer dangerous. Then she ran to Sawyer's side and dropped to her knees.

"Marc, are you all right?"

He had forgotten the pain of his wounded leg, of his shattered arm.

"Of course."

He tried to rise, and the leg folded under him.

Her hands on his shoulders would force him to sit quiet, but he refused stubbornly. His next try brought him upright, and he tested his weight gingerly on the injured leg. It held him. The bullet had torn through muscle, apparently, without touching bone.

"I'm okay."

She watched him closely, poised to catch him if he fell, and her voice trembled.

"I was at the fire. I rode back there to look for help, but no one would pay any attention to me. Then I heard the shooting up here and was afraid that it was you, that you were in trouble."

His grin was wry. "No one was ever in more trouble. I'd begun to think that your brother had a charmed life, that no bullet could touch him."

Her face grew more drawn. "That's what he used to tell us. He used to say that the man wasn't born who could kill a Kelly, that only another Kelly could do it."

She swung away, and he realized she was crying. She walked the few steps to where her brother lay and stood for a long moment looking down at him.

"I told Mother I'd look after you." She said it in a low voice, but the words carried to Sawyer. "I'm sorry, Joel. Someone had to stop you. I should have had the strength to stop you long ago. I didn't. I've paid for that lack of strength. I've stood all I can."

Sawyer watched her raise the gun, but for a full moment he did not comprehend what she was about to do. Then he jumped, forgetting his wounded leg, his crippled arm, in his sudden horror.

The leg gave way but not until it had carried him far enough so that his shoulder crashed into her side. They fell together, sprawling across Kelly's lifeless body, and the gun spun out of her hand in a small arc, to clatter against the front wall of the barn, six feet away.

She struggled to rise, and he caught her arm with his good hand.

"Let me go. Please let me go." She was near hysteria.

He sat up and drew her down into his arms, blocking her wild words with his mouth, pressing it hard against hers.

"Stop talking."

He felt the convulsive tremor run down through her small, rigid body.

"Please. I'll never have the courage again. I made some promises to myself when my husband died. I was going to track you down. I was going to settle with Joel, even if I had to kill him. I knew then I would kill myself. Do you know what it means to plan to kill someone who is very close to you, someone you have loved through most of your life, whom you still love in spite of the hatred you feel for him?"

Sawyer shook his head. He knew now that she had to talk, that this thing inside of her was like a cancer, destroying her, driving her.

"You see the way it is. You've got to understand. There isn't anything for us, Marc, there can't be anything. There are too many shadows, too many memories, memories I can't live down."

He kissed her again, this time with a fierce gentleness he had not known he possessed. When he had finished she was quiet, unmoving, in his arms.

He said then, with the same deep gentleness, "What about me?"

She pulled away from him, and in doing so saw the blood which now soaked the full length of his trouser leg.

"Marc. I didn't know it was so bad. The blood. We've got to stop the bleeding."

"It's all right. I've lost blood before."

"But not that much." She was thoroughly shaken. "And I've been worrying about myself. Have you a knife?"

He found his knife in his pocket and watched as she slit the cloth from hip to ankle.

She was all business now. She tore a strip from her petticoat, found a stick inside the livery doorway, and twisted a tourniquet into place above the oozing wound.

Then she swung toward her horse. "Don't try to move. I'm going to find a doctor."

"After you find the doctor, look up Paul Chum. They'll know at the railroad offices where he is. Tell him what's happened. Tell him to start riders after Kelly's men. Tell him to have Tupper picked up and held. Then come back and take care of me."

She stopped. She came back. She bent to take his good hand in both of hers.

"I'm a fool, Marc Sawyer. I was a fool to think I could kill myself and leave you. I knew it at the time." Her voice broke. "That's why I was in such a hurry."

He said, "The name isn't Sawyer. When you hear it you may not want to marry me."

"What is it?"

"Bill Smith."

She laughed, a small, flat sound that held mirth despite her emotional exhaustion.

"Bill Smith, I'd marry you if you had no name at all."

She kissed him then, slowly and fully, and he watched her ride up the street, erect, her head high, into the blowing smoke that now almost blocked out the brilliance of the rising sun.

John Hunter was the name used by Todhunter Ballard for a number of outstanding Western novels. Ballard was born in Cleveland, Ohio. He was graduated with a bachelor's degree from Wilmington College in Ohio, having majored in mechanical engineering. His early years were spent working as an engineer before he began writing fiction for the magazine market. As W. T. Ballard he was one of the regular contributors to *Black Mask Magazine* along with Dashiell Hammett and Erle Stanley Gardner. Although Ballard published his first Western story in *Cowboy Stories* in 1936, the same year he married Phoebe Dwiggins, it wasn't until *Two-edged Vengeance* (1951) that he produced his first Western novel. Ballard later claimed that Phoebe, following their marriage, had co-written most of his fiction with him and perhaps this explains, in part, his memorable female characters. Ballard's Golden Age as a Western author came in the 1950s and extended to the early 1970s. *Incident at Sun Mountain* (1952), *West of Quarantine* (1953), and *High Iron* (1953) are among his finest early historical titles, published by Houghton Mifflin. After numerous traditional Westerns for various publishers, Ballard returned to the historical novel in *Gold in California!* (1965) that earned him a Spur Award from the Western Writers of America. It is a story set during the Gold Rush era of the Forty-Niners. However, an even more panoramic view of that same era is to be found in Ballard's *magnum opus, The Californian* (1971), with its contrasts between the *Californios* and the emigrant gold-seekers, and the building of a freight line to compete with Wells Fargo. It was in his historical fiction that Ballard made full use of his background in engineering combined with exhaustive historical research. However, these novels are also character-driven, gripping a reader from first page to last with their inherent drama and the spirit of adventure so true of those times.